## "I don't dance," she said.

"Since when? I just saw you dancing at your parents' house."

Reluctantly, she swayed her hips under the sound of Beres Hammond's gentle voice. Watching her caused things to stir in Samson. He pulled her into his chest and they continued to dance. No words. He wrapped his strong arms around her waist, held her close. Soon she wrapped her arms tightly around his neck.

"The last time we were at the beach, things didn't go so well," she reminded him.

"Well, I'm hoping that this time will be different." He decided to go in for a kiss, and was glad that she didn't resist.

His lips touched hers gently, and the kiss was much sweeter than he'd imagined. His tongue found its way into her peppermint-flavored mouth. Her French-manicured fingertips danced their way across his face, caressed it. He held on to her waist. The strength of his arms made her feel safe. Wanted. Sexy. All the things she hadn't felt in a long time. Things she'd been too busy to feel.

Without a single word, he grabbed her hand and led the way back to the cabana.

Dear Reader,

You will appreciate Samson from the beginning. He's exactly what Alyson needs—someone to put her in check! He knows that she's all bark and no bite. With his tattooed arms and unshaven face, he's hardly her type. She likes her men a little more refined. Not to mention, he thinks he's God's gift to the world. She doesn't have time for that! She's too busy building her empire. But Samson isn't afraid to show her his worth.

If you remember Alyson from the first book in the Talbot series, you know that she's a bit uptight. She's the last one you'd expect to go trekking across the globe to Chicago (of all places) in the middle of winter, to get her man! But she's proof that love is worth going to the ends of the earth for.

I hope you will enjoy Samson and Alyson's story. And also the fantastical Christmas wedding of Jackson and Jasmine as they marry at the Grove. You'll get to see the warmth of the Talbot family again, and also become acquainted with Samson's spirited family. I hope you continue to love the Talbots. They are everybody's family!

Visit my website at monica-richardson.com or email me at Monica@Monica-Richardson.com.

Happy reading!

Monica Richardson

# A
# Yuletide
# Affair

## MONICA
## RICHARDSON

**HARLEQUIN**® KIMANI™ ROMANCE

Recycling programs
for this product may
not exist in your area.

ISBN-13: 978-0-373-86432-4

A Yuletide Affair

Copyright © 2015 by Monica Richardson

**⊕ HARLEQUIN®**
™ www.Harlequin.com

**Printed in U.S.A.**

**Monica Richardson** currently writes adult romances set in Florida and the Caribbean. Under the name Monica McKayhan, she wrote the Indigo Summer young adult series. Indigo Summer hit the *Essence* and *Black Issues Book Review* bestseller lists, and the series also received a film option. Monica's YA books have garnered accolades and industry recognition, including several American Library Association (ALA) placements on the Quick Picks for Reluctant Young Adult Readers and the Popular Paperbacks for Young Adults annual lists.

### Books by Monica Richardson

### Harlequin Kimani Romance

*Tropical Fantasy*
*An Island Affair*
*A Yuletide Affair*

Visit the Author Profile page at
Harlequin.com for more titles

For my Granny, Rosa A. Heggie
(November 1927–2008)
She was special in so many ways, and the
strongest woman I knew. My life is rich because of her.

## Acknowledgments

To my husband, the love of my life—
thank you for being my biggest encourager.
And for being my real-life hero.

To my family and friends—you are my support system.

To my readers that give me the energy to continue to
write, I'm sure you will enjoy the Talbot family and get
to know them well. I hope you will enjoy Alyson's story
just as much as Jasmine's. Thank you for your continued
support. Without you, our stories are just that, stories. But
through you, those stories come to life and take flight.

To my family in the Bahamas—visiting with you and
talking to you about my history has made the research
and writing of this Talbot series a complete joy.

# Chapter 1

Alyson Talbot hadn't planned on spending so much time in the Eleuthera Islands, Bahamas. She loved her family and her childhood home, but it was no place she had intentions of ever living again. In fact, she'd made a perfect home in Miami by purchasing a beautiful condo that overlooked the Miami River. Florida was where she needed to be—it was where she was building her clientele. After leaving a booming real estate company, she'd recently decided to branch out on her own, make a name for herself. Alyson Talbot and Associates wasn't quite where she wanted it to be, but the business was well on its way to making a statement in the industry. Just last year, she'd earned a decent salary, one that supported her comfortable lifestyle. But she was looking for more than just comfort, and her goal was to double those earnings in the coming year. She was certainly on a good track, and well on her way to accomplishing just that. She vowed to never move back to the islands nor help to run her family's B and B on Harbour Island.

Each of her siblings had vowed the same thing—that they would not be moving back to the Bahamas. Her oldest brother, Edward, was too busy working his political career and had ties to the mayor's office in Florida. Her brother Nate, who lived in Atlanta, was an artist and had no desire to run a B and B. And conversation around him moving back to the islands had always been a sore spot for him. Problems with a former girlfriend had limited his visits to their childhood home. Whitney was busy teaching small children at her Dallas elementary school and had claimed that she would return long-term, but hadn't. Their youngest brother, Denny, had already begun his tour of duty in the Bahamian military. He was the family's rebel, had opted out of attending college. Jasmine had been the only one to sacrifice and move back to the island. She had been instrumental in the Grove's renovation. But now that the family business was up and running, she needed help. Which was why she had turned to her older sister, Alyson. However, for Alyson, moving home was definitely not in the cards.

What *was* in the cards was helping to plan her sister's elaborate Christmas wedding. Without her contribution, Jasmine's wedding might not be as elegant as it could be. After all, she had connections, and people owed her favors. Not to mention, the Talbots weren't just an ordinary family anymore. They were more than just a two-parent family with six adult children scattered about the world. As owners of the Grove, the newest and fastest growing beachfront property on the island, the Talbots had quickly been placed in a league of their own. She knew that when the first member of the Talbot clan got married at the Grove, it had to be an event to remember. And it was up to her to make sure that happened—thus, causing her to spend way more time on the islands than she'd ever dreamed she would.

"Turn around and let me see the back," she told Jasmine, who modeled her seventh ivory dress.

It was a Vera Wang, and her sister looked like a model in it. She truly hoped Jasmine liked this one, because she was quickly running out of patience. She'd tentatively scheduled a meeting with an important client—a meeting that had already been postponed twice. She was committed to the wedding, but also had business in Miami.

"It's okay, but I don't get that warm fuzzy feeling about it. Mother said that I would know which dress was the right one. She said it would speak to me."

"It's a Vera Wang. What else would you like for it to say, honey?" Alyson asked. "Not only that, but our mother got married at the justice of the peace some thirty-plus years ago. What does she know about picking the perfect wedding dress?"

"That's just rude," said Jasmine.

"It's the truth, Jazzy!"

"Our mother may not have had the wedding of her dreams, but she definitely married the man of her dreams."

"I can't argue that."

Their father, Paul John Talbot, was a man whom both women cherished. Any man that walked into their lives had large shoes to fill.

"I want the dress to feel special," Jasmine insisted.

Her sister could wear almost any dress she wanted to, yet she made the task of finding a dress almost impossible. Jasmine had the perfect figure. Alyson wasn't nearly as fit as her sister, who worked out on a daily basis. She had to work hard just to maintain her ample figure. And as much as her patience was running thin, she had to keep reminding herself that this was not her wedding. In fact, she had no intentions of ever getting married. Marriage was overrated, and she hadn't had one single prospect anyway. She'd had her share of trysts and a few relationships that had lasted a month or two, but nothing serious. Her life was just fine the way it was, though.

"As much as I'd like to spend the day picking out bridal gowns, I think your husband-to-be is expecting us at the Grove pretty soon," Alyson reminded her sister with a quick glance at her watch. "He wants your input on the Caribbean band that's auditioning for the reception. I think we should head over there."

"Okay, just let me get out of this dress." Jasmine glanced at herself quickly in the mirror one more time and then grabbed hold of the silk train before stepping down from the platform.

"No love between you and that gown, huh?" Alyson asked again.

"Very little." She grinned and then disappeared into the dressing room.

Dress shopping with her younger sister was like watching paint dry.

Although it was still early November and Thanksgiving was forthcoming, Christmas had been the focal point at the Grove with Jasmine's impending wedding. The Clydesdale had already been decorated with gold, red and green lights streamed throughout. In the Grand Room, a huge, fifteen-foot Christmas tree stood tall in the corner of the room, garnished with garland, lights and unique ornaments. It was reminiscent of Alyson's childhood home in Governor's Harbour—a place where Christmases were an important part of her life. But more important than Christmas Day was the day after—Boxing Day. Boxing Day was when Junkanoo took place.

The festive street parade with music, dance and unique costumes was what dinner conversations were made of. Inspired by a different theme every year, it was the focal point of the Christmas holidays and the New Year, and it was the highlight of the year in the Bahamas. It took months to prepare for Junkanoo. There were costumes that needed to be made and feasts that needed to be prepared. When Alyson and her siblings were young, their father would take them to Nassau, where the largest Junkanoo parade took place. Although the Junkanoo parade in the Eleuthera was festive, nothing could compare to the one in Nassau. Now with the anticipation of a Christmas wedding, coupled with Junkanoo, the Talbot family were beside themselves with excitement.

The Caribbean band had set up their instruments in the center of the Grand Room and was playing an old Bob Marley tune. With locks that hung down to the center of his back, the band's lead singer danced around the room. Jackson, Alyson's brother-in-law-to-be, was so into the performance, he didn't even see them walk in. When he spotted them, a wide grin covered his handsome golden face as he bobbed his head to the music. He raised a glass of cognac in the air and motioned for Alyson and Jasmine to join him.

"You're just in time," Jackson said. "They're just getting started."

"They sound good," Jasmine said.

Samson, Jackson's friend, walked up and the two men shook hands. Alyson inconspicuously observed Samson as he chatted with Jackson. Didn't want him to notice that she was checking him out. She'd labeled him as the mystery man that had shown up on the island, with no real reason for being there. He was renting a room at their family's B and B for an extended period of time, and he'd been introduced as Jackson's buddy from college, but her knowledge of him was very limited. The lack of information intrigued her.

"Why don't you play something?" Jackson asked Samson, and then told everyone in the room, "He's an accomplished guitarist."

"I'm an amateur at best," Samson insisted.

"He's being modest," Jackson countered. "Get on up there and give us a little something."

Reluctantly, Samson joined the band at the center of the room. The band's guitarist handed over his instrument, and Samson began to play. Alyson tried desperately to peel her eyes from his sexy face, and she'd never intended to focus so intently on the way his lips curved when he was in his zone. She certainly didn't mean to stare at his muscular arms, or the way the sleeveless shirt hugged his chest. With his tattooed arms and unshaven face, he was definitely not her type. She preferred her men refined and sophisticated. But she couldn't help but be impressed by the way he played the guitar and how he meshed perfectly with the other members of the band.

*Get yourself together, girl*, her inner voice whispered. *What in the hell is wrong with you?*

She didn't have time to watch this man play a guitar! He wasn't even in the band—he was a wannabe. And what was he doing in the Bahamas, anyway? The nuptials weren't taking place for weeks, and he wasn't even an attendant in the wedding.

"I don't need to see anymore. I think this is our band for the reception," announced Jackson. He then turned to Jasmine. "What do you think, babe?"

"Bravo!" Jasmine clapped her hands as each member of the band took a bow. "I agree."

At least she agreed on something, Alyson thought as she raised an eyebrow at her indecisive sister. "How about deciding on a wedding dress, boo?" She'd said it aloud before realizing the words had actually come out of her mouth.

"Don't start, Alyson." Jasmine pointed a finger at her sister.

"No luck finding a dress today?" Jackson asked Jasmine.

"She's going to be wearing that tablecloth if she doesn't choose a dress soon," Alyson teased.

"I really don't care what my bride-to-be is wearing on that day, just as long as she meets me at the altar and becomes my wife like she promised." Jackson grabbed Jasmine from behind and gave her a tight squeeze.

The two moved to the sound of the Caribbean music. Although Alyson rolled her eyes, secretly they gave her hope that love actually was attainable. She was happy for her sister and wished her a lifetime of bliss with the man of her dreams. The two sisters had only recently hashed out their differences and gotten over old wounds, and Alyson was grateful that they were able to put the past behind them. And she was happy to be an integral part of her sister's life and wedding plans.

"What's the story on your friend over there?" Alyson asked the question that had plagued her since the day Mystery Man had shown up in the Bahamas.

"He's my college buddy," Jackson said.

"Old information. I gathered that days ago," she told him. "I mean, what's his story?"

Jackson placed an arm around Alyson's shoulder. "What exactly would you like to know about him?"

She pulled away and exclaimed, "I'm not interested in

him, if that's what you're insinuating! I'm just curious as to why he's here. Normal people have careers and families that prevent them from relocating to a tropical island for an extended period of time."

"He's just here for a little while. Needed to get away."

*Get away from what?* she thought as she gave Samson another quick glance.

"What happened in Chicago?" she asked.

"Maybe you should ask him yourself," Jackson said as Samson finished the set and walked up.

Samson gave Alyson a dazzling grin and nearly pierced her with those seductive light brown eyes. He gave her a nod of hello.

"You're far from a novice, boy. You're a professional." Jackson grinned and gave Samson a strong handshake. Then he turned to Alyson. "I'd like for you to meet my future sister-in-law, Alyson Talbot. Alyson, this is Samson. I don't think I've had the chance to formally introduce you two."

"Pleased to meet you, Samson." She offered her hand.

He took it and gently kissed the back of it. "The pleasure is all mine."

She quickly retrieved her hand from the man who'd instantly caused her to feel things—*strange things*—that she shouldn't feel when meeting someone for the first time. Samson smiled, apparently completely aware of his effect on her. She rolled her eyes. He was trying too hard, and she wanted him to know that he didn't stand a chance with her. Maybe if she were a twenty-two-year-old groupie, his charms would work. But she wasn't twenty-two, nor was she one of those desperate women who threw themselves at the feet of charming men, and he needed to know that. She'd always been one to sift through the smoke screen and get to the heart of the matter.

"Talbot women certainly are beautiful," said Samson.

She noticed the word *Toni* etched across his left biceps, and asked herself, *Who has the names of their ex- or current girlfriends etched into their skin*?

"Alyson is a real estate broker," Jackson offered. "Her company is quickly becoming the go-to for real estate on the island and abroad. You mentioned taking a look at some beach homes while you're here. Maybe she can show you around."

Alyson gave Jackson the evil eye and then looked at Samson. "I generally don't dabble in the competitive market. But I have a lot of connections and would be happy to pair you with one of my associates who could show you around."

"I think she just told me that I can't afford any of the properties in her portfolio but she'd pawn me off on someone who can show me some cheaper ones." Samson smiled, and the entire room seemed to illuminate.

"I think she did," Jackson agreed.

"What is it that you do for a living, Mister…"

"Steel."

"You steal for a living?" she asked.

He and Jackson both laughed a hearty laugh.

"My name is Steel. Samson Steel," he said.

"Oh." She felt silly, but offered a gentle smile. "The most modest home in my portfolio, Mr. Steel, appraised at half a million dollars last week. We're asking much more than that."

"Great! I'd like to see it."

He was wasting her time! Between helping to plan a wedding and juggling appointments with clients in Miami and the islands, she didn't have time to play games with Samson Steel. She pulled a business card from her purse and handed it to him. "My website is on there. Why don't you peruse the homes on my site and see if there's anything that you're interested in? Save us both a lot of time and effort."

He studied the card. Flipped it over. "So I can reach you at this number?"

"If necessary," she said.

"Is it your personal cell, or will this take me to voice mail?"

"I don't do voice mail, Mr. Steel. My clientele is way too important for that. I have a personal assistant who handles all of my calls."

"Ah, I see," he said thoughtfully. "I'll give you a call in the morning. Maybe you can fit me in tomorrow afternoon."

"Can't tomorrow. Early afternoon, I have an appointment with a client. And then right after that, I'm scheduled to taste wedding cake with my sister."

"Um, Alyson... I meant to tell you that we'd rescheduled that appointment for Friday," Jasmine chimed in. "The bakery called this morning."

"When exactly were you going to tell me?" she attempted to whisper.

"I called Jules and had her check your schedule, and she penciled you in for the tasting on Friday. So it looks like you're free tomorrow afternoon...to show Samson some properties..." she caught Alyson's wicked glance "...*or not.*"

"Call my office tomorrow, and I'll try to fit you in." There was no way out of this one.

"I appreciate that, Alyson Talbot." He smiled widely again. "I'm looking forward to you fitting me in."

He shouldn't get it twisted, she thought. This would be strictly business.

# *Chapter 2*

No doubt, he was enigmatic—it kept people at arm's length. It allowed him to share only what he wanted others to know. He'd come to the Bahamas where the only person he knew was Jackson Conner, his buddy from college. They'd met at Harvard and had kept in touch over the years. Though they hadn't spoken every day, he considered Jackson to be a good friend. And he was shocked to learn that Jackson had abandoned his hometown of Key West, fallen in love with a Bahamian girl and taken up residence in the Caribbean. His friend had always been a city fellow. A contractor, Jackson had owned a successful business in Florida and had built some of the finest properties that Samson had ever seen. That is, until meeting Jasmine Talbot.

It was Jackson whom Samson called on the phone that day when life seemed unbearable.

"I never thought you'd leave Florida. And I'm surprised

that some woman has snagged you and taken you toward the altar!" Samson had told Jackson.

"I never thought I would, either," said Jackson, "but love has a way of rearranging your entire life."

"I wouldn't know. I'm an eternal bachelor."

"Yep, I thought I was, too," said Jackson. "You just need to bump into that woman who will turn your world upside down."

"I've had plenty of women turn my world upside down, for a good twenty, maybe thirty minutes." Samson laughed. "And then I'd roll over and fall asleep."

"I'm talking about for life, not just in the bedroom," Jackson said. "You should come over here for a visit, man! It's the best place to clear your head after everything that's happened. Besides, I'd really like for you to be here for the wedding."

"Jackson Conner's getting married," said Samson. "Wow!"

"It's not that far-fetched," Jackson said. "Now you, on the other hand, you're afraid of marriage."

"I'm not afraid of marriage. I just don't think it's necessary. There are too many beautiful women out there to settle down with just one." Samson sighed. "But that's just the world according to Samson. Obviously you have a different opinion about it, bro."

"I absolutely do. And you will, too, someday. Some little honey is going to snatch your ass up one day, have you making her an omelet wearing nothing more than an apron and your birthday suit."

They both laughed. It had been months since Samson had joked like that. There hadn't been much to laugh about.

"I can't live without her. I had to make her my wife." Jackson was more serious then. "She changed my life."

"I'm truly happy for you, Jax man. I wish you the best."

"What about you? What's your next move?"

"Don't know."

"Come over here for a few weeks," Jackson had insisted. "Relax a bit. Get a new perspective."

"I don't know, man."

"I'll have Jasmine hook you up with a room at the Grove," Jackson said emphatically.

The Grove was a trio of old homes that had been transformed by Jackson's construction company into beautiful beachfront properties. Each home had its own distinct personality, theme and name. Ironically, Samson had chosen to stay in the home that happened to share his name, Samson Place. It was tranquil and bold, much like him. Decorated in Caribbean colors—pink, blue and yellow—Samson soon found his temporary home there. After settling in at the Grove, he'd resolved to only return to Chicago when his head was clear, and not a day before.

When he'd first laid eyes on Alyson Talbot, he thought she was beautiful. Her hard exterior was a dead giveaway. She was able to fool everybody else, but he had her figured out from the beginning. She was insecure. He flirted because...hell...he was a flirt. Samson was charismatic and loved women—and they loved him. He knew he'd never settle down with any of them for any significant length of time anyway. So he had fun—enjoyed life. Not because he had a fear of commitment, but because he knew he'd never find everything he wanted in one woman. It was impossible.

As beautiful as Alyson Talbot was, she wasn't his type. In his opinion, she was snooty and judgmental—two qualities that he wouldn't tolerate. He'd already read her, and had met a million other women just like her in his lifetime. And concluded that she'd been hurt by someone in her past, which was why she'd decided to take it out on every man alive. And that, he didn't have time for. He was too busy healing his own wounds, which was why he was in the Bahamas to begin with.

He sat on a stool, the acoustic guitar resting on his leg, his fingertips fretting the strings. He closed his eyes for a moment. Listened as the music resonated through the room. It was a beautiful love song, and the band's lead singer sang the Caribbean ballad with confidence. When Samson opened his eyes, he caught Alyson eyeballing him from across the room. Her eyes were focused on him, and his on her. For a brief moment he thought she was feeling him. That is, until she seemed to realize she'd stared too long, and looked away. She began toying with her phone.

She was dressed in business attire, and he doubted that she even owned a pair of sweatpants or jeans. She probably didn't dress down very often. Always on guard, always prepared, regimented. A pair of black slacks hugged her ample hips. A gray jacket barely contained her generous bosom. He thought she was sexy as hell, with long flowing hair, high cheekbones and a gorgeous, fleeting smile.

He wasn't interested in settling in the Bahamas, but he was interested in getting in between Alyson Talbot's thighs. If spending time with her meant he had to look at beautiful properties along the island's coast, then he'd entertain it. Contrary to what she believed, he could own just about any property he wanted on the islands. He'd invested his money well and had built quite a nest egg. He had money and could afford any of Alyson's properties, but it wasn't real estate that he was interested in at all. Besides, he was sure that the island life wasn't for him. After all, he was a big-city man with big-city hopes and dreams. And the thought of living on an island seemed too constricting.

Chicago had been his home all of his life. He grew up in Hyde Park. His grandfather Conrad Steel had served for many years as a Chicago police officer before retiring. His father, Cecil, had followed in his footsteps, and joined the force at a young age. Becoming a police officer had never been Samson's dream, and even with the pressure of preserving the family's tradition, he chose law instead. He'd attended the University of Chicago on a music scholarship, with hopes of becoming an accomplished guitarist. However, an undergraduate law class had changed all of that. Becoming a lawyer was inevitable at that point.

He hopped down from the stool and handed the acoustic guitar back to its rightful owner. Shook hands with every member of Onyx, the band that had welcomed him like an old friend. He talked music for a few minutes with the band members and exchanged phone numbers. He laughed with them as they all promised to get together again.

"I'm thinking you should play with us at the wedding," said Justice, the band's guitarist. "I have an extra guitar."

"I think that would be great," the lead singer, Kosmo, agreed.

"I brought my own guitar with me. It's in my room." He rarely traveled anywhere without his cherished instrument, affectionately known as Bailey. "But I don't think I'm quite ready to play at the wedding."

"Why not?" asked Kosmo. "You're no amateur."

He looked across the room at the spot where Alyson had stood playing with her phone. She was gone.

"You were absolutely wonderful," said Bijou. Her gentle hands caressed his back, as if it was the most natural thing in the world for her to do. The Caribbean beauty had been a beast on the drums. With copper-colored eyes, a petite frame and a head filled with curly tresses, Bijou was drop-dead gorgeous.

"Thank you. You're quite the musician yourself. How long have you played?"

"All my life," she said, and then changed the subject. "How long will you be on the island?"

"I haven't decided yet." It was an honest answer.

"Maybe I could take you on a tour of the island. Show you around a bit."

"So you live here?" He disregarded her invitation. Needed time to absorb it.

"I'm here in the Eleuthera temporarily. I'm from Cat Island. Are you staying here—at the Grove?"

"Yes, I am."

"Good! I can pick you up tomorrow evening. I'll show you some of the best beaches on the island." She wasn't shy at all. "Wear your trunks."

He was intrigued by her wickedly sexy smile. A cropped top revealed toned abs; a silver ring pierced her navel. Tight denim shorts hugged her hips, and revealed a set of smooth, cappuccino-colored legs. A heart-shaped tattoo played peekaboo on the inside of her right thigh. Samson couldn't wait to kiss his way from that heart all the way up to her sweet spot.

"I'll wear my trunks," he flirted. "Will you be wearing yours?"

She moved closer in, brought her lips to his earlobe and whispered, "I usually don't wear anything at all when I swim."

She walked away, moving her hips from side to side. He watched her, admiring her round ass. She must've known he was watching because she turned around and gave him a grin and a wink. He exhaled.

"Damn," he whispered to himself.

"I'm only going to have a small window of time tomorrow." Alyson startled him as she walked up from behind. "I'll meet you at the water ferry at three. Not a minute after. Not three fifteen. Not three twenty-five. I don't like being late, and I will not wait for you to arrive. You have my business card—call if you need to cancel. My time is valuable. Please don't waste it."

She was walking away before he had an opportunity to respond. Her round hips moved to their own music. He thought that watching Bijou walk away was nice, but watching Alyson walk away was downright delightful.

# Chapter 3

Alyson thought Samson was a musician and a drifter, and couldn't afford the guesthouse of some of the properties in her portfolio. However, she'd managed to find a few condos and a villa that she thought might be in his price range and fit his tastes. She arrived at the water ferry a few minutes early, stood on the dock and answered a couple emails on her phone.

Butterflies stirred in her stomach as she waited for him to arrive. She pulled a small compact from her purse and checked her hair and makeup, *again*. She'd spent too much time preparing for this encounter. Way too much time. And she didn't like what she was feeling. She was nervous, and for no good reason. As strong and as independent as she was, her knees still felt somewhat weak when she was in the presence of Samson Steel.

Well, that was yesterday. Today would be better. She'd exhibit more strength. He wouldn't make her feel vulnerable again. She wasn't his type anyway. She saw the way he gawked at that young girl in the band—the drummer with the small waistline, skinny legs, exposed flat stomach. He looked all goo-goo eyed. If he liked slight girls, then Bijou was more his type, not her.

She sent a text message to the owner of one of her listings, Jennifer Madison: I have a strong buyer for Madison House. All cash. Full price offer. Quick closing.

Jennifer replied after a few moments: Great. Send over the contract and I'll take a look at it.

I'm also showing it this afternoon.

The Madisons weren't any ordinary family. Jennifer Madison's father had built a successful real estate development company. They were a prominent family that owned homes on Miami's Palm and Fisher Islands, as well as properties along the coast in the Bahamas. But of all the houses that they owned, the Madison home was Alyson's baby. It was her first listing that even came close to a million dollars. Her firm had listed plenty of homes on the islands, but she'd personally nurtured this one. It was by far her most expensive listing yet, and was sure to net her a substantial commission—one that would change the financial face of Alyson Talbot and Associates. A sale of that magnitude would earn her the business of every one of Jennifer Madison's rich friends and associates. She desperately needed it.

The pant legs of her linen Armani suit blew in the wind. Her recently pedicured toes peeked through her shoes, and she'd worn a professional-looking blouse but made sure she showed just a little cleavage—just to tease Samson a bit, show him what he couldn't have.

He stepped out of a taxi wearing denim shorts, brown leather sandals, a snug gray T-shirt and a gray plaid newsboy cap on his head. He was clearly dressed down, but he even made dress-down look sexy. His perfectly manicured beard caused him to have a strong resemblance to Omari Hardwick. Alyson found it difficult to peel her eyes from his muscular, tattooed arms. She thought it ridiculous for any human being to defile their body in such a way, but there was something tantalizing about Samson's body art. She looked away. Didn't want him to catch her staring. He didn't deserve the satisfaction of knowing that she thought he was one of the sexiest men she'd met.

He paid the driver and then headed her way.

"You made it on time," she said.

"Better than that. I'm five minutes early," he boasted.

She looked at her watch, and then up at him. His arms were folded across his chest, and a smirk danced in the corner of his mouth.

"That you are." She avoided eye contact.

"Good seeing you again, Alyson. I appreciate you fitting me into your busy schedule."

She ignored his greeting and instead ran down their plans for the day. "We're going to take the water taxi over to Governor's Harbour. There are a few houses I can show you over there. They aren't as elaborate, but I'm sure they would fit into your price range."

"You don't even know what my price range is. You haven't asked."

"You're a musician. And not a professional one. I admit I'm being a bit presumptive, but—"

"I'd say you're being extremely presumptive," he said. "Is this how you handle all of your clients, or just the ones you devalue?"

"Are you telling me that you can afford a property that costs more than two hundred thousand dollars?"

"I'm telling you that you never gave me the courtesy

of asking what my price range was. You assumed that I couldn't afford the properties in your *portfolio*," he mocked her. "Isn't there a process to this? Shouldn't there be standard questions that you ask a potential client?"

"I do have a few questions, Mr. Steel. Like, what are you doing in the Bahamas for an extended period of time? What are you running from? Do you have a woman or a baby mama in the States who's chasing you for child support?"

"Those are really inappropriate questions," he said.

"I apologize. I think we got off on the wrong foot." She handed him a sheet of paper from her briefcase. "Here's a list of properties that I thought you might be interested in. If this is not your price range, we can adjust."

He took the list and gave it a quick review. Handed it back to her. "Actually, I brought my own list."

He reached into the back pocket of his shorts, pulled out a folded piece of paper and handed it to her. She opened it. Gave it a quick scan.

"These properties are close to a million dollars!"

"Your point?"

She ignored his question. "And besides, the Madison property already has a buyer."

"That's the one that I'm most interested in. I saw it on your website this morning. It was the only one that had a video. You should do that with all of your properties, by the way…add a video. Excellent selling point. And your website didn't indicate that that property was sold, by the way."

"I just spoke with the owner this morning, and she's waiting for me to send over the contract right now." Why was she explaining this to him? "I already have a solid offer on it."

"But you haven't accepted that offer yet, right?"

"Well…"

"I would like to see the place."

"Why would I show you a property that's not for sale? And if I thought for one second that you could afford it, I couldn't show it to you today anyway. It's on Abaco—over a hundred miles from here. It would take us too long to get there by boat."

"I don't have anything but time."

"It would be a complete waste of time."

"It's not the only property on Abaco that I'm interested in. There are others in the same general vicinity."

"We don't have transportation."

"Actually, we do. Jasmine told me that your cousin Stephen owns a boat, and he often transports you between the islands. She even gave him a buzz, and asked if he was available today. He was more than happy to oblige. So what's your excuse now?"

He was right. Their cousin Stephen was very accommodating whenever she needed use of his boat. Often if his schedule permitted, he'd drive Alyson between islands to meet with clients and show properties. But she didn't need her sister planning her day for her, or telling Samson Steel all of her business. She'd address that with Jasmine the next time she saw her.

Sooner than she would have liked, Stephen pulled the boat to shore and tied it to the dock. He waved for them to come along. Alyson gathered herself and walked toward the boat. Samson followed closely behind.

She wasn't sure what the day would bring, but so far she wasn't pleased with its start.

# Chapter 4

On *Sophia*, Stephen's powerboat, they traveled at a fast pace across the Atlantic Ocean. Stephen steered the boat through the clear turquoise waters. Alyson reclined on the leather seat on the port side of the boat, behind Stephen, while Samson relaxed in its bow. His back was to her, so she had an opportunity to check him out without his knowledge.

Samson and Stephen chatted about everything under the sun—whatever it was that men chatted about. Occasionally she'd tune in to the conversation, which didn't really amount to anything more than a conversation about the ocean, deep-sea diving and the Islands of the Bahamas. Stephen was a diver, and boasted about it every chance he got. He'd go diving for fish and lobsters. Stephen told Samson about his and Alyson's upbringing. As first cousins, they spent a great deal of time together as children and even as teens and adults. The Talbots were a close-knit clan.

When they arrived on Abaco, Stephen tied a rope from the cleat of the boat to the dock. He helped Alyson climb out of the boat first, and then helped Samson.

"I have a couple that I'm taking on a sightseeing tour," Stephen said. "Shouldn't take me more than an hour, Chicken."

Chicken was a nickname that she'd never outgrown. It was a name that clearly didn't describe her, as she was not afraid of anything. However, some of her family members saw fit to give it to her anyway, and she hated it.

"An hour? Are you kidding me?" she asked. "Why didn't you tell me you had business on Abaco before you brought me here?"

"Alyson, this is my livelihood. I always schedule other business when we come here. You know that. I have to take advantage of every opportunity to make money."

Stephen was definitely an entrepreneur. He owned a rental shop along the beach on the Eleuthera, where he rented jet skis and surfboards by the hour. He used his powerboat to transport tourists between the islands. Though Alyson often complained, she appreciated him allowing her to tag along on his moneymaking trips. But because he was her younger cousin, she felt obligated to give him a hard time—each and every time. It was a habit that she hadn't quite grown out of. She didn't care about Stephen leaving her for an hour, but spending time alone with Samson was what she feared most.

"Hurry back." She kissed her cousin's cheek. "I need to get back to the Eleuthera before nightfall. I have an early meeting that I need to prepare for."

"Good luck with her," Stephen told Samson. "She's impossible to deal with."

"I'm not impossible! I'm just a woman who knows what she wants."

Stephen shook his head, and then stood on the deck. Lit a cigarette. "I'll call you when I'm on my way back."

Madison House was one of the most alluring properties in the Abacos. Positioned at sixty-eight feet above sea level and overlooking the Sea of Abaco, the magnificent beauty boasted six bedrooms and a great room all connected by massive breezeways. Each bedroom had its own private balcony. The vaulted ceilings, Brazilian wood flooring and the glass walls were by far the main attractions. The view of the beach from the great room was stunning.

"There are no words to describe this property," said Samson. "I don't think I've ever seen anything more beautiful."

"You like, huh?" she asked.

"It's breathtaking."

Samson followed her across the mahogany floors and into the kitchen with its upscale stainless-steel appliances and a dumbwaiter. French doors off the kitchen led to a porch that wrapped all the way around the property. She stepped outside and felt the tropical air against her face— breathed it in.

"I could live here." Samson said it softly.

"Unfortunately it's not for sale. But since you insisted on seeing it, here it is," she told him.

"Here it is, indeed."

They stepped back inside and took the winding staircase to the second level and to the master suite. Huge glass French doors led to an enormous private balcony with a view of the ocean.

"This is unreal," said Samson.

It took them more than thirty minutes to finish the tour. When they were done, she set the alarm and secured the property.

"We can use the golf cart from this house, and I'll drive

you over to a nearby property. Of course it's a little more quaint, but still very beautiful."

"I'll follow your lead," he said.

They drove the golf cart along the road to a smaller three-bedroom house on Marsh Harbour. Tall palm trees greeted them in front of the well-manicured yard.

"This one seems a little more practical," Samson said as they entered the home. "I like the kitchen. It's much bigger than the other house."

"Why would you care about a kitchen?"

"I cook. And very well, as a matter of fact."

"And what is it that you cook?" she asked with a bit of skepticism in her voice.

"A little of everything, but mostly soul food. Collard greens and the best fried chicken you've ever tasted," he boasted. "I make a mean sweet potato pie, too."

She looked at him. "You make sweet potato pie?"

"A mean one," he insisted.

"That's my favorite pie. I can eat a whole one all by myself."

"Well, maybe I'll make you one someday," said Samson. "Do you cook?"

"All my life. Mostly Bahamian dishes. Our mother made sure we all learned how to cook. Said the quickest way to a man's heart is through his stomach." She laughed. "Not that I care about getting to a man's heart. But it's nice to know how to cook, nonetheless. At least I'll never go hungry, right?"

"Why aren't you interested in getting to a man's heart? Aren't you interested in men?"

"Of course I'm interested in men." She set her purse down on the kitchen counter. "But I'm just not interested in the whole drama of a relationship right now. Don't have the time or the energy. My life is fine just the way it is."

"Relationships don't always have to bring drama. Maybe you're unhappy by your own choosing."

"I never said I was unhappy! I'm quite happy, in fact." She was convincing herself more than him. "But I'm just not interested in the whole drama of a relationship right now. Don't have the time or the energy. My life is fine just the way it is."

"Relationships don't always have to bring drama. Maybe you're unhappy by your own choosing."

"I never said I was unhappy! I'm quite happy, in fact." She was convincing herself more than him. "But what about you? You have a wife, girlfriend or baby's mother back in…wherever it is you came from?"

"Chicago. And none of the above. I'm a happy bachelor."

"So you live in Chicago?"

"Southside."

"What part?"

"In a historical, black neighborhood. A lot of culture there."

"Isn't there also a lot of crime?"

"Not any more than anyplace else. And where do you live, on Miami's Fisher Island somewhere?"

"Downtown."

"Should've known."

"What do you mean, 'should've known'? I'll have you know that downtown Miami is very cultural. A lot of history there, as well," she explained. "And why do you live in Southside Chicago, anyway?"

"It's my home. I was born and raised there. It's where I grew up. I'm proud of my home. I envy your upbringing. Must've been nice, growing up in the Bahamas."

"It was restricting. I outgrew this place. Quickly!"

It had been years since she'd lived on the islands. A native of the Bahamas, she'd gone away to college and vowed never to return to the islands permanently. And even after the completion of her family's bed-and-breakfast, the Grove, she still had no desire to return. However, visiting properties with Samson caused her to remember why she loved the Bahamas so much. It was still her home, where her family lived, and still one of the most beautiful places in the world.

Her father was a retired physician, and he was the best example of what she wanted in a man. Genuine and caring and very intuitive, he was part of the reason she'd never settled down with anyone. No one could ever compare to him. That and the fact that her mother's voice was forever in her head about everything. Her mother's little anecdotes and lessons lived in her mind. She didn't know why she listened to her mother, though. Beverly Talbot had done the opposite of what she constantly encouraged her daughters to do. She told them to follow their dreams, when she'd abandoned her own dreams only to follow their father's.

"Sometimes in life, we make sacrifices, Alyson." That had been her mother's excuse. "I wanted a better life for you guys. That's why I didn't follow my dreams."

Alyson and her siblings had certainly benefited from their mother's sacrifices. Their parents had somehow managed to put every one of them through college. Everyone except for Alyson's youngest brother, Denny, who'd chosen the military instead. He was currently away completing officer's training in the United States. The rebellious one with a mind and style of his own, he'd certainly been the exception to the Talbot family rule.

Somehow he'd also managed to weasel his way out of working for their family's business. The Grove was their inheritance—passed down to them from their grandfather Clyde Talbot. They each had a stake in the business. Jasmine had been the first to move back to the islands to oversee the construction of the family's B and B. She'd written the business and marketing plan. And after the renovation had been completed by her fiancé, she'd been instrumental in hiring staff and overseeing the day-to-day operations.

But Jasmine was becoming overwhelmed. Their youngest sister, Whitney, a schoolteacher in Texas, had made promises that she would move back home after the school year ended, but so far that hadn't happened, and Jasmine needed help. Planning a wedding and running the Grove was certainly taking its toll on her. As a result, Alyson found herself on the islands more often than she wanted to be. It had been weeks since she'd been to her home in Miami.

"If we're done looking around, I should lock up."

"I'm done," said Samson.

Her phone buzzed, and she pulled it out of her pocket. It was a text message from Stephen.

Taking a bit longer than expected. Might be another hour...maybe two. Sorry ☺

"Really, Stephen!" she said aloud.

"What?" Samson asked.

"He said he might be an hour or two longer," she explained. "I apologize."

"Don't," said Samson. "Let's just make the best of it."

"How?"

"There's a beautiful beach a few steps from here. I say we take advantage of it."

"I say we don't. I'm not even dressed for the beach."

"When was the last time you just let your hair down?"

"I can't remember. I don't have time to let my hair down."

"Well, today you will." Samson grabbed her hand and ushered her out of the kitchen and through the living room, straight to the front door.

"Just let me lock up."

* * *

Samson didn't waste any time removing his hat and laying it atop a huge rock. He pulled his T-shirt over his head, and all Alyson took in were golden brown abs and strong arms and the beautiful sunshine beaming against smooth skin. He removed the leather sandals from his feet and headed for the water. He didn't even bother to remove his trousers before jumping in for a swim.

"The water's warm!" he yelled.

"That's nice."

"Why don't you take your clothes off and come in?"

"Imagine that," she said, and then decided to remove her leather pumps.

The last thing she needed was to ruin a perfectly good pair of Manolo Blahnik shoes. Never mind that she'd caught them on clearance at a Saks end-of-season sale. Still, they weren't cheap! And she would not be removing her clothes in front of a man that she barely knew. She was appalled that he would even suggest it.

She rolled up the legs of her pants, tiptoed through the sand and moved closer to the water. Samson was doing a backstroke in the water. He was moving farther away from the shore, and she feared that he was being careless.

"Hey!" she called. "You shouldn't swim so far out."

He smiled and waved and continued to swim farther out. Soon he disappeared, and she couldn't see his head. Her heart pounded as she moved closer, and soon she was standing in the water.

"Samson!" she called again.

No response and no sight of him. She pulled her cell phone out of her pocket. She quickly tried to dial 911, but her fingers were shaking.

Samson had swam farther out into the deep part of the ocean. She was breathless when she didn't see him anymore.

A Jet Ski zoomed past, and she tried flagging it down. They waved as if she was saying hello, and kept moving. She crept farther into the water. As she pressed the numbers on her cell phone, it slipped from her grasp and fell into the water.

"Shit!" she exclaimed and crouched down to pick it up.

She missed seeing the wave that suddenly crashed against the shore *and* the side of her face. It soaked her hair and clothing with one splash. She inhaled deeply and attempted to catch her breath. Then she tried turning her cell phone on.

"Looking for someone?" Samson popped up out of the water, startling her.

"Are you crazy?" She swung at him, but he grabbed her hands. Restrained her.

"What is wrong with you?"

"I thought you drowned!"

"Well, I didn't." He grinned. "I'm glad to know that you cared, though. You were willing to save my life?"

"Let go of me! You are so twisted! And this is definitely not funny!" she yelled. "You're an asshole! My phone probably doesn't work anymore, and my hair is wet and my clothes are soaked!"

"I'm sorry. I didn't know that you thought I was drowning. I was fine. I'm a swimmer."

She rushed angrily to shore. Samson followed, attempting to express his sorrow. Her clothes and her hair were ruined, and she was livid. Stephen couldn't return to the island soon enough, she thought. Samson Steel had certainly burned his bridge with her, and there was no recovering from this.

# Chapter 5

The weather in the Bahamas was beautiful—warm and tropical—but it was as cold as ice on the boat ride back to Harbour Island. Samson glanced back at Alyson, who was seated on the port side of the boat. She'd managed to pull her wet hair back into a ponytail. Her clothes were wrinkled and drenched. A pair of overpriced shoes rested next to her on the seat, and a set of earbuds was inside her ears. He wondered what she was listening to, but dared not ask. He was just grateful that her phone still worked.

"She'll be okay." Stephen caught him checking her out.

"I didn't know she thought I was drowning. I went out a little deeper than I probably should have," Samson tried to explain. "And she should've seen me swimming back to shore."

"She said she wasn't looking…too busy trying to get her phone to work. But I tell you what… I wished I'd have seen her rushing out into the water like that. I bet that was a sight to see." Stephen laughed.

"Why doesn't she date?" Samson asked.

"Oh, she dates," said Stephen. "She just doesn't commit. She's afraid of letting someone in. Whenever someone gets too close, she runs them away."

"Dealing with her seems like so much work."

"Alyson Talbot *is* a lot of work. But I believe when the right guy comes along, she'll let him in."

Samson glanced at Alyson one last time. Her eyes were closed this time.

The trio reached Harbour Island by nightfall. Samson helped Stephen guide the boat to the deck and secure it with a rope. Stephen helped Alyson climb out, and then he helped Samson. She never looked his way, just stomped toward a bench and sat down, folding her arms across her chest.

"Give me a minute and I'll drive you both to the Grove," Stephen said.

"Don't worry about it. I'll take a cab!" Alyson snapped.

Samson Place was decorated in tropical colors—pink and turquoise. It was tranquil and oozed with romance. It was the sort of place where lovers retreated for long weekends. He watched as Alyson spoke briefly with the young woman at the front desk. The woman handed her a key, and she breezed right past Samson, walking briskly toward the wooden stairwell.

"I'm sorry, Alyson." It was his last attempt at penance.

"Don't worry about it," she said and kept walking.

With a long sigh, he pulled his room key out of his pocket and headed for his room, as well.

"Where have you been?" Samson recognized the voice immediately. Bijou wore a bikini top and a pair of cutoff jeans. Flat stomach, silky smooth legs and leather flip-flops. Her toes were painted in a hot-pink nail polish that matched her bikini top. "I've been looking everywhere for you! Did you forget?"

"Forget what?" he asked.

"That we had a date, silly." Her breasts were perfectly round and buoyant. "Remember, I was going to show you around the island?"

He didn't think they'd actually set a date. In fact, he thought they were just making flirtatious small talk. "Was that today?" he asked.

"You did forget." She pouted.

"I can't today, Bijou. I'm sorry."

"Oh, no, mister!" She grabbed his arm. "I'm not letting you renege."

He couldn't believe he'd actually agreed to the rendezvous. And there was little he could do to get out of it, so he followed Bijou to an old pickup truck parked in front of Samson Place. Bijou jumped into the driver's seat and slammed the door shut. Samson reluctantly walked around to the other side of the truck, hopped into the passenger's seat and slammed his door shut. She started the engine, and although the rusty Chevy was in desperate need of a paint job, the engine hummed like it was brand-new. He held on to the door handle as Bijou peeled away from the curb. She tuned the radio to a Caribbean party station and turned up the volume as loud as it would go. He held his breath as she sped through the streets of Harbour Island. He barely heard as she pointed out some of the island's landmarks. His mind was elsewhere—on Alyson and the anticipation of making amends with her.

"Let's go for a swim!" Bijou pulled up at the beach without warning.

"Let's not," he told her. "I didn't bring any trunks."

He didn't need trunks, but had no desire to take a swim

with Bijou. He'd had his fill of swimming in the ocean for one day, and it hadn't gone well at all.

"Don't you want to go skinny-dipping?"

What man wouldn't want to skinny-dip with a beautiful woman like Bijou? He'd be crazy not to.

"Maybe another time," he said. "You think you could drive me back to the Grove now?"

"You're putting me off." She poked her lip out.

He didn't have an answer, and couldn't believe he was turning down an opportunity to skinny-dip with a beautiful woman. His buddies back home would be giving him the side-eye, wondering if he'd grown soft.

He managed a smile. "Rain check?"

Bijou wasn't giving up without a fight. She untied the strings of her bikini halter top and dropped it. Her breasts sprung to life. He noted that they were a beautiful shade of brown with perky nipples. Her fingertips reached for his face, caressed his temples. She grabbed his hand and slipped his index finger into her mouth. "Still want to go back to the Grove?"

"Those...are...very beautiful." He breathed in deeply. There was no denying he was aroused, but he stood his ground.

He didn't know when it happened, but Alyson had become his new endeavor, and getting her attention had suddenly become his focus.

"Glad you like them." She smiled seductively.

"Please put your top back on."

"Was it something I said?" she asked. "I was too forward."

"It's not you. It's me." He sounded like a cliché, but he didn't care. He had no desire to impress Bijou. "It's just that I need to get back and speak with someone."

"With that woman—Jasmine's sister. The stuffy one," she said matter-of-factly. "It's too bad she has such a bad attitude."

"She's beautiful, though," Samson rebutted.

"She's a bit overweight."

Samson laughed at Bijou's cattiness. He thought her jealousy was cute. Alyson was far from overweight, in his opinion. She had curves in all the right places. He thought she was sexy as hell, and couldn't seem to get her out of his head. Bijou lifted her bikini top back up and tied it around her neck again. She started the truck, put it in Reverse and peeled out of the sand at full speed. He wasn't sure she was able to drive at a normal pace, or even move at a normal pace, for that matter. A man usually had to work hard for what she was willing to give so freely. *Fast* was definitely her middle name. A week ago, he'd have appreciated Bijou's audacity. Women had always been his weakness. He couldn't think of anything better than a beautiful woman's body pressed against his. But his priorities were suddenly beginning to change.

In an attempt to drown the uncomfortable silence in the truck, Bijou turned up the stereo as loud as it would go. He gazed out the window to keep from looking her way. He wanted to apologize to her, but couldn't find the words. He just needed to be back at the Grove, and it seemed he couldn't get there soon enough.

He found Alyson in the common area at Samson Place. She was reclined on the tangerine-colored antique sofa, pecking ferociously on the keyboard of her laptop. Instead of approaching her immediately, he found his way to the kitchen. Raquel, one of the Grove's Bahamian cooks, stood in front of the stove with an apron tied around her generous hips.

"Can I get two cups of tea, please?" he asked.

Raquel stopped stirring something in a huge pot, just long enough to look at him. "She likes green tea, with a splash of lemon and just a drizzle of honey," she said in her sweet Bahamian accent.

"You mean Alyson?"

"Yes, Miss Talbot is very specific about her tea, amongst other things," she said as she placed a fire beneath the tea-kettle and grabbed two large mugs from the mahogany cabinet. "And how do you like your tea, Mr. Steel?"

He wondered how she knew his name. It seemed that everyone around the island had become fully acquainted with him.

"I'll have mine the same way as hers, I guess."

"She's mad. You know that, right?" Raquel asked. "You messed up royally."

"You heard her mention it?"

"The whole house did." Raquel shook her head. "Came in here ranting and raving about her time being valuable, and her clothes and hair being ruined."

"Wow," he said.

"Just be yourself, and apologize profusely."

"You think that'll work?"

"I've known the Talbots for a long time, and it wasn't that long ago that I changed Alyson's diapers." Raquel smiled. "She has a hard exterior, but the truth is, she's a real softy on the inside…if you can manage to get in there."

"I don't see anything soft about Alyson Talbot, except maybe…" He caught himself, realized that he'd said too much. "Never mind."

"Now, see, that's what's wrong, Mister Steel. You got your priorities all mixed up. Thinking with the wrong head. You're out gallivanting about town with Bijou, doing

God only knows what, and now you want to make amends with Miss Talbot. Such a man!"

"I didn't… I mean, Bijou and I didn't…"

"I don't want to hear any of the details, honey. You just need to make up your mind as to what it is that you want."

"You know a lot about things, Miss Raquel."

"I know about everything that goes on around here," she told Samson.

Samson laughed. Where he was from, there was a name for people like Miss Raquel—*nosy*. Once the teakettle whistled, Raquel made green tea with splashes of lemon and drizzles of honey and then sent him on his way.

"Now go. Be persistent. No woman wants a mouse of a man."

"I'm not a mouse, Miss Raquel. I'm far from that."

"Well, good! Because she's strong and needs someone to take charge. And don't take no for an answer." She didn't smile, but gave him a nod. "Now, go on, child."

"Thank you."

He cautiously stepped out of the kitchen and headed toward the area where Alyson was engrossed in her computer. He placed the mug on the rustic coffee table in front of her. "Just the way you like it," he said.

She stopped pecking on her keyboard for a second, looked up at him and then at the cup. "And how do you know how I like it?"

"I have my sources."

"Raquel has a big mouth." She began typing again.

"I need you to accept my apology. What I did was juvenile and thoughtless." He plopped down in the chair opposite the sofa.

"Already forgotten." She grabbed the cup and took a sip. A look of satisfaction briefly appeared on her face.

"Could've fooled me. You keep giving me these looks of disgust—scowling at me."

"Maybe it's your own imagination. Don't give yourself so much credit," she said.

"So you're not scowling at me?"

"Nope," she lied, and then changed the subject. "Did you enjoy your evening?"

"You mean my tour of the island? I did indeed."

"And I'm sure you enjoyed your beautiful tour guide, as well."

"Bijou is a nice girl."

"I agree. Hopefully she doesn't get taken advantage of by the likes of you."

"What's that supposed to mean—'the likes of me'?"

"Playboy, philanderer. You choose the term."

"I love women. That's not something I can argue. In some circles I might be considered a playboy, if you will." He wasn't helping his case very much. "But right now I have my sights on one woman—and one woman only."

"And who might that be?"

"The one who's giving me the hardest time, who won't let things go."

"I don't dwell on things, Mr. Steel."

"Then have dinner with me tomorrow evening. Give me a chance to redeem myself."

"I can't."

"Of course you can. You have to eat. Rock House at seven. I'm not taking no for an answer. Be there at seven. And don't be late." He stood and headed for the stairwell before she had an opportunity to run down a hundred excuses why she couldn't make it. He took Raquel's advice and stood his ground.

Raquel was peeking out from the kitchen and gave him

a wink as he passed. He gave her a wide grin and then headed up to his room. Didn't even turn to see the expression on Alyson's face. He was sure she was astounded.

## Chapter 6

Friday morning, and she'd almost forgotten that she'd committed to tasting wedding cakes with her sister.

"I don't know who he thought he was, barking orders at me as if…" Alyson stuffed a fork filled with red velvet cake into her mouth "…oh, my God, that's good!"

"I'm partial to the white Amaretto. And oh, Lord, the chocolate Bavarian crème is simply delightful." Jasmine took a forkful of her sister's red velvet and tasted it. "But oh, this red velvet."

"I'm telling you right now, Jazzy, I am not at all interested in that man!" Alyson eyeballed the baker who sat across the table from them. She tried to lower her voice to a whisper. "He's so…so…egotistical."

"He seems very nice and genuine to me," Jasmine countered. "And you have to admit he's gorgeous. Isn't he?"

"He's a womanizer. Already running about town with that young woman from the band."

"Bijou? Oh, she's much too young for him. And not at all his type."

"Could've fooled me. And what would you know about his type? Do you even know this man?" Alyson asked her. "Does Jackson even know him? I know they claim to be friends, but how long has it been since he's seen him last?"

"They've been friends for years. And Jackson knows him very well. He's a great guy, Alyson," Jasmine said. "You should give him a chance."

"I don't trust him." Alyson licked cream cheese frosting from the side of her finger. "What does he even do for a living?"

"Well, as I understand it, he was an assistant district attorney for years. But recently he decided to run for mayor, and there were some issues that surfaced with his campaign. I don't know all the details, but I understand there was a little scandal of some sort. There were rumors that he'd accepted some bribes. Somebody had it in for him."

"See, that's exactly what I'm talking about! Scandalous."

"None of it was true," said Jasmine. "But he was so devastated, he decided to come over here to clear his head and regroup."

"You mean run away from his troubles."

"That's not what I said, Alyson. And I think you should stop being so judgmental. Give the man a break. Go to dinner! Find out who he is for yourself."

"Not interested," said Alyson. "And I'll let him know that no one gives me orders. No one!"

Alyson pulled out her cell phone to check the text message that had just come through. Jennifer Madison wanted to know why the full-price offer on Madison Place had fallen through. She didn't have the nerve to tell her that the buyer had changed his mind—found another home that suited him better. She needed the property to sell, and she needed it to happen soon. She had bills looming over her head.

"Thank you for filling in for Jackson today, sis. He hates that he's not able to participate in all the little details of the wedding." Jasmine grabbed Alyson's hand. "But I'm so glad you're here."

"Me, too." Alyson smiled. "But don't get used to me being here all the time, Jazzy, and I mean it. My life is in Miami. And I have a business there, too."

"I know. I know. But I'm just glad you're here now."

"I'm leaving on Monday. Have an early flight out," said Alyson. "You should come with me. Maybe we can visit a few bridal boutiques, look at some dresses. Maybe you'll finally fall in love with one."

"I might take you up on that. Jackson won't be back until next Friday."

"We'll leave on the first flight out in the morning," Alyson said. "I'll have Jules check rates for you."

"We'll be back by the week's end, right? We're having our family dinner next Saturday. Did you forget?"

She hadn't forgotten. Family dinners at the Talbots' home weren't an option. You were expected to be there when you lived as close as Florida. Their siblings who lived in Atlanta and Texas were given a pass. And their youngest brother, Denny, who was training in the Royal Bahamas, would also be absent. But Jasmine, Alyson and their brother Edward, who also lived in Florida, were expected to show up.

"I didn't forget," Alyson said. "How could I when Mother has reminded me every single day this week that I'm preparing the macaroni and cheese."

"Macaroni and cheese? You got off easy," said Jasmine. "I'm doing the conch salad and conch fritters."

"It's because you still live at home. You get all the grunt work." Alyson laughed. "Maybe once you move into your own home, you'll get some relief."

"It's so hard living with them sometimes. Always keeping tabs on me as if I'm still a kid. But with Jackson working and traveling so much, I prefer to be there with them. It's better than being alone in some empty house."

"You'll be a married woman soon. And maybe your husband will quit working so much and spend more time at home, so you don't have to spend so much time with the old people." Alyson laughed. "Sitting on the porch listening to Daddy's stories of the old days."

"I love Daddy's stories." Jasmine giggled.

"I bet you don't have an ounce of privacy. And how many nights do they sip on sky juice and play George Symonette albums?"

Both women laughed. While they enjoyed contemporary Caribbean artists, they knew that their parents still preferred old-school calypso and goombay music styles. It was what they knew and loved, and what the Talbot children grew up listening to.

"Every Saturday night I'm listening to George Symonette while Mother dances around the room, a highball in her hand. Daddy has to pry the glass from her and put her to bed," said Jasmine. "She's sipping on the sky juice more often these days."

"She's worried about Denny," Alyson said. "He should've gone to college like the rest of us."

Beverly Talbot hadn't been the least bit happy with her son's choice for his future. She'd particularly made a fuss when she learned that her baby boy would be shipped away to the US to be trained with the navy SEALs.

"He followed his heart," Jasmine defended Denny. She'd

had many conversations with him about his choice. He'd been brave, in her opinion.

"The rest of us didn't have the luxury of following our hearts," said Alyson, "except maybe you, when you went tramping off to California looking for the next acting and modeling gig."

"I try to forget about that. That was before the Grove," said Jasmine. "The Grove changed my life."

"I have to admit that you have grown up quite a bit since the Grove. You've done a fantastic job with the place," said Alyson. "I'll be honest with you, Jazzy. I didn't think you could pull it off."

"I'm sure you weren't the only hater." Jasmine laughed and threw a napkin at her sister.

Alyson threw it back. "I'm not a hater."

"You are," Jasmine exclaimed. "That's why you won't give Samson a chance."

"What is it with you and this fellow?" Alyson groaned. "He wants me to go to dinner with him tonight and give him another opportunity to mess things up."

Jasmine shook her head and took another bite of white Amaretto. "Stop being a stick-in-the-mud! Love is a wonderful thing."

"Who said anything about love? I'm talking about dinner, which I won't be attending."

"I think you should open your heart and be prepared for whatever comes your way."

"Not this time. An open heart is an open door for pain."

"Not always."

It had been in Alyson's life. Every man that she'd ever opened her heart to had left it broken. And she wasn't up for taking the risk. She loved herself, and that was love enough.

Alyson changed the subject. "I like the red velvet. It's super moist. Melts in your mouth!"

"I love the red velvet, too. It's delicious, and also festive. Perfect for a Christmas wedding," said Jasmine. "I think it's a winner."

"Good, then we're done here." Alyson stood. "I really need to get going. I have phone calls to make...paperwork to complete."

"You can run along while I finish up here." Jasmine stood and gave her sister a strong embrace. "Thanks for coming."

"My pleasure, Jazzy," Alyson said. "I'll have Jules book you on my flight in the morning."

"I'll be packed and ready to go."

"Good. I'll see you tomorrow."

"Let Samson know that you're accepting his dinner invitation."

"I can't. I have too much going on."

"Open your heart for romance."

"Goodbye, Jazzy." Alyson waved her sister's comment away as she exited the bakery.

# Chapter 7

The condo was a bit stuffy, having been closed up for several days. Alyson opened the kitchen window and breathed in the Miami air, then opened the refrigerator and pulled out a bottle of water. She had roughly an hour to shower, dress and meet her clients at the title company in Fort Lauderdale. Their flight from the islands had been delayed, causing her entire schedule to be pushed back.

Jasmine relaxed on the sofa, the remote control in her hand as she flipped between channels.

"You're welcome to tag along, but you'll be bored out of your wits," Alyson said.

"I think I'll stay here and relax a bit." Jasmine curled her feet beneath her bottom.

"I'll bring lunch," Alyson said before disappearing into the bedroom.

After dressing in a fashionable suit, she rushed to her convertible BMW, slapped her briefcase against the leather seats and affixed her Michael Kors sunglasses onto her face. She looked at her reflection in the rearview mirror, dabbed lipstick on and smacked her lips together to work it all in. She snapped her seat belt on and slid a CD into the console. The Caribbean rhythm filled the car. The convertible top eased its way down as she slowly pulled out of the parking garage. She hated being late, but could probably make up some time once she made it to the interstate, provided she could navigate through rush hour traffic.

Traffic on I-95 inched along slowly, and she leaned her head against the back of the seat. She found herself daydreaming about a certain wannabe musician, with a gorgeous smile and tattooed arms that had become surprisingly enticing to her, even though she denied her attraction to him, dismissed any possibility of spending time with him. She had shunned him and his dinner invitation. Had she gone, she would have relinquished her control. And she needed to be in control of her own destiny. It had been a while since she'd given any man the time of day.

Carl had been the last straw. He was almost her father's age, but she'd tried not to notice the age difference. They'd shared the same interests—the theater, museums and exotic restaurants, something that most men her age weren't at all interested in. Men her age were still partying at the South Beach clubs. Carl was different. He was laid-back and conservative. And just when she'd started to develop feelings for him, she discovered that he was still married to the mother of his grown children. His very angry wife of twenty-two years had shown up at the restaurant where they were enjoying a candlelit dinner, and accused Alyson of being a home wrecker.

It was the last time she'd let anyone into her space. There was no time or room for a relationship. Her life was overloaded with shaping a new business, all the while trying to maintain a certain lifestyle. If she didn't grow her portfolio soon, she'd be forced to sell her beloved condo and downsize to a cheaper place. Selling the Madison property on Abaco would help her stay above water. Her real goal was to connect with Jennifer Madison's father, who was a commercial developer. There was a larger profit in commercial properties, and she wanted a piece of it. Jennifer had promised Alyson an introduction, but an introduction didn't guarantee a business deal. It would be left up to her to sell herself to the real estate mogul.

Her phone rang through the speakers in her car. She picked up with the click of a button on the car's dashboard.

"It's Alyson."

"If you're en route to the title company, don't bother," her assistant said. "The buyers can't close."

"What do you mean?"

"Changed their minds last minute."

"They can't do that!"

"They did, honey. Just got off the phone with their Realtor," said Jules. "They don't care about losing their escrow. They've decided to move to New Jersey to be closer to their grandchildren."

Alyson sighed. "Didn't they know they had grandchildren in Jersey before putting a contract on a home in Florida?"

"Apparently so, Alyson. But they didn't know they wanted to live closer to them."

"Or that they were wasting our time!" Alyson exclaimed. "Get on the phone with the sellers and schedule a time for me to meet with them. We've got to get this property back on the market right away. We're losing money every moment it's off the market. Try to schedule it as soon as possible because I'm heading back to the islands by week's end."

"Your afternoon is free, so I'll try to set it up for today."

"Thanks, Jules." She disconnected the call.

She got off at the next exit and headed back toward Miami. She drove down Calle Ocho to Versailles, a Cuban eatery in the heart of Little Havana, to grab a café cubano and a couple of empanada pies with spinach and cheese inside. She passed on the pancakes and syrup that normally accompanied her empanadas. Watching her weight had its sacrifices. Her hips were nicely shaped, but a few too many pancakes might take them to the next level—a level that she really didn't want to go to.

She loved Miami's Cuban community. Little Havana reminded her of home. It was her way of having a little bit of Caribbean without actually having to return to her childhood home permanently. It was home to some of her favorite indulgences—the little eatery that sold the best Cuban sandwiches, the Latin theaters and Domino Park, where she would occasionally stop and gawk at the old men as they competed against each other in a game of dominoes. She grabbed a copy of the *Miami Herald* and headed back to her downtown condo.

"I brought breakfast instead of lunch," she told Jasmine.

"What happened?" Jasmine followed her sister into the kitchen.

"My clients canceled," she said. "I brought coffee and empanadas."

"They look and smell delightful," said Jasmine, who didn't hesitate to dig in.

"Enjoy!" Alyson said as she exited the kitchen.

"You're not having any?"

"I'm watching my weight."

"Since when?" Jasmine yelled.

"Since now!"

Lately she'd become more cognizant that her clothes were fitting a bit more snug than she wanted them to, and something needed to change. She stepped into the extra bedroom that had been transformed into a minigym, dusted off the treadmill and stepped onto it. She found an upbeat playlist on her phone and turned up the volume as loud as it would go. She took long strides, with her spandex exercise pants hugging her hips. Her mind unintentionally drifted to Samson, and how fit he was. She wasn't sure why thoughts of him were suddenly crowding her small space, but there he was, creeping his way into her thoughts *again*. Although she hated to admit it, she admired his confidence.

What she exhibited to the world was poise and self-assurance, but underneath she was all but. She was afraid that she wasn't good enough, smart enough. That she might fail at building Alyson Talbot and Associates into a successful business. She feared that she might spend the rest of her life alone because she was too rigid, too judgmental, too independent, and if she wasn't careful, too damn fat for a man to give her a second look. She needed to feel good about herself again. She wasn't overweight, but didn't feel good about her body. She wanted to be fit, like her sister who worked out on a daily basis. And like Bijou, the woman whose body she secretly envied.

The Beyoncé track was interrupted by a call from Jules. She placed it on speakerphone.

"I've scheduled for you to meet with the Tuckers tomorrow afternoon. It's the only time they were available."

"That's fine. Thanks, Jules."

"Why are you breathing like that?" asked Jules. "You okay?"

"I'm on the treadmill."

"You mean the one that's been collecting dust since you bought it last year?"

"I don't need the judgment."

"No judgment. Do your thing, girl." Jules chuckled.

"Whenever you're done, let me know," said Alyson.

"I'm done," said a much more composed Jules.

"Good. I need you to book my sister and me a flight back to the islands tomorrow afternoon—sometime after my meeting."

"Going back so soon? I thought you weren't going back until the weekend."

"Change of plans."

"You and Jazzy going shopping for dresses?"

"Yes, sometime this afternoon. And she better find one today because I'm headed back to the Bahamas tomorrow!"

"Why the urgency? Your family dinner isn't until Saturday."

"I just… I need to go back," Alyson said. "Something's come up."

"Fine." Alyson could tell Jules wanted to pry, but didn't. She knew Alyson very well. They'd been friends long enough to know when something was different. She would find out what it was soon enough. "I'll take care of it."

"Keep it within the budget. We're watching every dollar."

"I know," said Jules. "We'll get there, sweetie. Pretty soon, Alyson Talbot and Associates will be a household name."

"Damn right it will! And you'll get your old salary back."

"I'm not worried about that. I'm living with Mama right now, so my expenses are a lot less these days. My stress level is through the roof, though. That woman is hard to live with. But at least I'm saving money."

"I appreciate you hanging in there with me."

"Don't mention it. I wouldn't be anywhere else. I'm invested."

"You're the best."

"I know!" Jules said with a giggle. "Now go finish pretending to exercise."

"I *am* exercising. I've got another mile on this thing."

"Knock yourself out."

Jules believed in Alyson, and knew that it was just a matter of time before she was on top again. Alyson loved Jules like family. They'd met in college. A native of Miami, Jules was the first person to embrace the young girl from the Caribbean, who was away from home for the first time and knew nothing about the United States. They became instant friends. After college, Alyson landed a job at a large real estate company. Jules was an accounting major, but struggled to find work. Alyson hired her as a part-time personal assistant, just until something came along. Jules had been with her ever since.

After a few miles, Alyson hopped down from the treadmill. She took a long hot shower and slipped into her favorite pair of designer jeans—the ones that boosted her self-esteem because they hugged her in all the right places. She needed all the boosting she could get.

Later that afternoon at a local bridal shop, Jasmine stared at her own reflection in the mirror as Alyson sipped a glass of red wine. She had prepared herself for a long day of dress shopping with her indecisive sister. Her heart skipped a beat when she saw Jasmine step up onto the platform wearing the soft white strapless organza gown with dramatic ruffling at the bottom. The pewter-colored ribbon hugged her sister's small waist. She was speechless for a moment.

"What do you think, Jazzy?" Alyson finally asked.

Jasmine took her time about turning around, but finally faced her sister. She had tears in her eyes. "This is it," she whispered softly.

"Are you sure?" asked Alyson.

"I'm sure," said Jasmine. "This is it."

"You look absolutely beautiful!" Alyson gave her sister a warm smile. She stepped up onto the platform and adjusted the ribbon on Jasmine's dress. Took a quick glance at the price tag. "Damn, sixteen hundred dollars. I hope Daddy's sitting down when you call him."

"I thought you would make the call, Maid of Honor."

"That was before you exceeded your budget by four hundred dollars," said Alyson, "and that's not really a maid of honor duty."

"You know this is the gown, Alyson. It's so beautiful!" Jasmine gushed.

"It *is* beautiful, but I'm not doing your dirty work." Alyson pulled out her cell phone, dialed her father's number and pushed the phone into Jasmine's hand. "Daddy's on the phone."

Jasmine rolled her eyes and took the phone, rushing into the dressing room. Alyson knew their father wouldn't put up a fuss. He would do just about anything for his children, and especially his daughters. If this was the wedding dress that Jasmine desired, she knew that it would give him great joy to buy it for her. The dress had been worth the wait, and Alyson was relieved that her sister hadn't settled. Though she was grateful that the long search was now over.

Jasmine rushed from the dressing room, still wearing the gown. "Alyson, we have to get back to the islands. Daddy had a heart attack!"

# Chapter 8

Samson knew CPR, but had only administered it one other time. When a client went into cardiac arrest right there at the courthouse, he had revived her and called for emergency help. He thought he'd have to do the same thing for Paul John Talbot. The senior member of the Talbot clan had been visiting the Grove, looking for his daughter Jasmine. Samson was having tea in the living area at Samson Place when Paul John approached him and introduced himself.

"You must be the friend of Jackson's that I've heard so much about." Paul John held out his hand.

"Yes, sir. I am."

"Good to meet you. Have you seen either of my two daughters around here?"

"If I'm not mistaken, I believe they took a flight to Miami this morning," said Samson.

"Miami, huh?" He laughed a little.

Samson remembered thinking that Mr. Talbot didn't look well. He looked fatigued.

"Are you okay, sir?" he asked.

"Yes, just a little tired," said Paul John. "I wish these girls would tell us when they're leaving for the States. It's good information to know. If something happened to them, my wife and I wouldn't know anything. Jasmine packed a bag, but I thought she was staying here at the Grove for a few days. Didn't know she was leaving the country."

"Anything I can do to help?"

"Just let them know I was here, looking for them."

As soon as Paul John turned to leave, he grasped his chest and bent over. He grabbed the arm of a chair for balance. Samson rushed to his side and helped him to sit down. Paul John held on to his chest and seemed to experience light-headedness and shortness of breath. Samson attempted to hide the fact that he was panicking. He pulled his phone out, but wasn't quite certain how to call for an emergency on the island.

"I'll call the police station," yelled Raquel, who stood nearby. "They will dispatch an ambulance."

After making the call, Raquel rushed back to the living area. She handed Paul John two baby aspirin. "Here, take these, Mr. Talbot...chew them. It'll help."

He took the aspirin, stuffed them into his mouth and began to chew. Samson felt as if he was losing control, wasn't sure what to do. He was grateful to hear the roar of the ambulance's engine as it pulled up in front of the Grove. The emergency volunteers emerged from the vehicle, rushed inside and began medical treatment.

"We're going to take him in. Would you like to ride?" one of the volunteers asked Samson.

He didn't know what to say, but nodded.

"I'll call Mrs. Talbot!" said Raquel.

Samson climbed into the back of the ambulance and took a seat right next to Paul John. As the vehicle zoomed through the streets of Harbour Island and the sirens wailed, Samson began to pray. The ride seemed long and agonizing. It felt as if they wouldn't make it to their destination in time, and he'd witness something he wasn't quite prepared for.

Finally the ambulance pulled up in front of the Harbour Island Ministry of Health, and the volunteers rushed Paul John inside. Samson stayed in the lobby, pacing the floor. Praying for a miracle. He pulled out his phone and dialed Jackson's number. No answer. He left a detailed message, and then plopped down into an old chair. Dropped his face into his hands. He felt helpless and hated feeling that way. His stomach churned, and his heart began to beat a fast pace. He checked his watch, and then checked it again.

When the older woman walked in, he knew that she was Alyson Talbot's mother because she looked like an older version of her. With a flawless brown face and long, graying hair, she was a spitting image of the woman he thought of more often than he should. She rushed in to see her husband. And later, when she returned to the lobby where Samson paced the floor, he barely knew she was there.

"What's your name, baby?" she asked.

He turned to greet her. "I'm Samson."

"I'm Beverly Talbot," she said. "I understand you've been right here with my husband all morning. And you're responsible for getting him here."

"Yes, ma'am."

She hugged him. "You are a godsend."

"I'm glad I was able to help. How is he?"

"He's going to be just fine. He's resting now," she said. "Paul John has a hard head. I struggle to get him to watch his cholesterol. And he's a physician, too. He should know better."

"I'm glad I could help, Mrs. Talbot."

"You're Jackson's friend from the States?"

"Yes, ma'am."

"So nice to meet you," said Beverly. "Would you please join us for dinner at our house on Saturday?"

"I would be honored," said Samson.

"Good. Five o'clock." She smiled. "And bring your appetite. My daughters and I are preparing a Bahamian feast."

"Thank you."

She placed the palm of her hand against his face and gave him a warm, motherly smile. She reminded him of his own mother, and how he missed her. When she rushed back to be with her husband, Samson pulled his phone out of his pocket and dialed his mother's phone number.

"Ma, it's me."

"Samson, why are you calling me? You know these international rates are outrageous. You should've sent me an email, or a message on that Faceplace thing."

"It's Facebook, Ma, and you don't even visit your page. And I wanted to hear your voice," he said. "How did it go today?"

"I nailed it!" She giggled. "That damn parallel parking almost messed it up for me, though. But I did it. I got my license."

"I'm so proud of you."

"You should've seen me, Sammy, adjusting my mirrors and carrying on. And your daddy let me use the Chrysler. Can you believe it?"

"I can't believe it. He's anal about that car."

"Damn right he is! And you know how bullheaded he can be. Not wanting me to get my driver's license. It might've taken me thirty years, but I was determined. And I did it."

"I love you, Ma."

"I love you back," she said. "What do I hear in your voice? What's going on?"

"Nothing," he lied. "Just missing my favorite girl."

"Oh, shoot, I'm fine. Now tell me about the Bahamas. Are they anything like the pictures I've seen on television?"

"Better. It's absolutely gorgeous over here."

"Are you staying out of trouble?" she asked. "You've got to stop playing the field, Sammy. Find a nice girl and settle down."

"I will, Ma. One day." He knew that he needed to end the conversation before she went into her spiel. "You need some money?"

"You know I don't need your money, son. I'm doing just fine."

He'd saved his money and invested in the stock market. He'd done well. A single man with no children, Samson had more expendable funds than he knew what to do with. Early in his career, he made sure he took care of his aging parents. He knew they would never consider leaving their two-story brick home where he grew up. No, that was not an option. So instead, he'd renovated it for them—had beautiful hardwoods installed, fresh paint throughout, and all new appliances to replace old run-down ones. He'd set up a bank account for them—a place where he would deposit cash for them on a regular basis. That was before the scandal.

After the scandal, his father insisted that he shut the bank account down. "We don't need your dirty money."

It was a punch to Samson's gut, but he pretended not to be bothered. For so long, he'd lived for the approval of his father, whose footsteps he hadn't followed. And his father often reminded him that he wouldn't be in the predicament that he was in had he not followed his own path.

Samson was from a long generation of cops. His grandfather had been a police officer for over thirty years, and his father's career had been nearly as long, with twenty-nine years on the force. His older brother, Jessie, and his younger brother, Calvin, were both officers. Samson was the only one who'd taken a different route. He'd gone to the University of Chicago and then to Harvard Law School. He had no desire to chase criminals through Chicago neighborhoods. Instead, he preferred to try their cases before a court of law. He'd landed a job in the DA's office shortly after graduation.

When he decided to run for mayor, his mother had been his strongest supporter. She'd worked diligently on his campaign, putting in long hours, raising money and answering phones. She was proud of her baby, and didn't care one bit that he hadn't become a police officer. The job was way too dangerous for her taste anyway. She worried herself sick about her other two sons who spent their days patrolling the streets of Chicago, and didn't mind one bit that one of her sons had chosen a different path.

Samson was her hero, but in his mind she was one of the bravest people he knew. She'd endured chemotherapy, and the cancer had been in remission for the past two years. Yet she never missed a beat. Even when the treatments left her exhausted and sick, she kept fighting, always caring more about the next person than her own faltering health. He was so proud of her that he'd had her name etched across his biceps in bold letters, *Toni*. It was a reminder that when things got tough, her bravery was his strength.

"If you need anything, you let me know," he told his mother.

"I need a new daughter-in-law, is what I need. And some grandchildren."

"You have a daughter-in-law. Jessie's wife. And they have a kid," Samson teased. "And Calvin has a kid. Last time I checked, you had two grandchildren."

"You know what I mean, boy," Toni said. "I want you to settle down."

"Something's going on with my phone. I think we have a bad connection. Hello. Hello."

"Okay, bad connection, Sammy Steel," she said. "You just remember that time doesn't wait for anyone."

"I love you, Ma."

"Yeah, I love you, too," she said. "I'm going to have Calvin scan my driver's license so I can send you a copy by email."

"That would be nice."

"Are you coming home for Christmas?"

"I don't think so. Jackson is getting married on Christmas Day, and I want to be here," said Samson. "I've unofficially joined the band that was hired for the reception."

"Unofficially, huh?" His mother chuckled. "You got your guitar with you?"

"Of course."

"That's always been your first love. I'm glad to see you're staying true to it."

"Always."

"Send pictures of the wedding."

"I will."

"And, Samson." She hesitated. "Take care, baby."

"You do the same, Ma. I'll call you again soon."

He hung up, but held the phone against his chin. He missed her more than he realized. He missed her almost as much as he missed seeing Alyson Talbot's face around the Grove. She'd only been gone for a short time, and he already missed her presence. No doubt, she was under his skin. Which was odd, because he didn't allow women to get under his skin—he was always in control. Women chased him, not the other way around. He couldn't remember the last time he had been the chaser.

But he was chasing this time, and she was running. And he intended to figure out why. His original intent was to get her in bed, but something had happened along the way. She intrigued him, and he wanted to know everything there was to know about her.

## Chapter 9

Samson was quite fond of Bailey, his acoustic guitar made of Sitka spruce with its rosewood fingerboard. He rarely went anywhere without it. He rested it on his leg, and his fingertips quickly began to fret the strings as he joined Onyx while they performed their Caribbean Christmas medley. He'd never heard Nat King Cole's "The Christmas Song" played quite like that. He felt nervous as a crowd gathered in the Grand Room to listen to the band play. They sipped wine and other cocktails and danced to the music. Some of them sang along, while others nibbled on hors d'oeuvres. Soon the crowd had grown bigger than he expected. It seemed that every guest staying at the Grove was in one room.

He was surprised to see Alyson's face in the midst of the crowd. Dressed in a business suit, with her arms folded across her chest, her lips curved into a slight smile. He gave her a wide grin and a wink. She blushed, unfolded her arms and began to move to the music a bit, trying to ignore him. After the news of her father's heart attack, he'd expected her to return from Miami soon. And he was pleased to see her. Couldn't wait to finish the set and work his way over to her.

"Look up," he whispered in her ear as he held the mistletoe above her head.

She looked up, and he kissed her cheek.

"How dare you kiss me in front of all these people?" she whispered. "And it's not even Christmas yet."

"Close enough. And you didn't seem to mind." His smile was intoxicating.

"Are you always this full of yourself?"

"Always," he said.

"I'm glad you're here." Suddenly they seemed like old friends. "I wanted to thank you for what you did for my father. You saved his life, and I am eternally grateful."

"I didn't do anything I wouldn't have done for my own father. I just went with him to the clinic."

"It was a big deal to my family," she said. "And to me."

"Maybe you can repay me with dinner."

"Maybe I can," she resolved.

"How about tonight?"

"The Rock House, I suppose," she said with a smile.

"Yes."

"I'll meet you there."

"Good." He said it casually, but could hardly contain his excitement.

He decided to walk away, leave before she changed her mind or came up with an excuse. He walked back toward the band and prepped for the next song. The anticipation of getting to know Alyson Talbot beyond her business suit and professional disposition caused him anxiety, but music always calmed his fears. He was enjoying himself in the islands, and was grateful for the recess from his life in Chicago. He wanted to forget about it, at least for now.

It had been a while since the trial, and he should've been proud of how he'd single-handedly won convictions against mayor-elect Conrad Phelps and William Blue, owner of Blue Island Properties, who had paid Phelps thousands of dollars to get their bids approved. Blue Island had funded Conrad Phelps's campaign, in exchange for him getting all of their development plans approved once he was in office. And Mayor Phelps had kept his promise.

They'd been suspected of wrongdoings for years, but the corruption continued. Finally the FBI conducted a real estate sting that brought the racket to its demise, and ultimately Mayor Phelps, several city employees, William Blue and several of Blue Island's employees were arrested. Samson, as assistant district attorney, was successful at bringing charges against them all. However, he wasn't aware of the consequences involved in solving an agelong case. For years, evidence had been *overlooked* because the mayor and Blue Island had ties that were much bigger than the FBI. It wasn't long before Samson realized just how deep those ties ran.

After the convictions, Samson had become somewhat of a hometown hero, and running for mayor quickly went from a fleeting idea to an attainable goal. He had plenty of supporters and soon left the DA's office to begin raising funds for his campaign. However, in the midst of his campaign, all hell broke loose. Suddenly, he'd been accused of accepting bribes—the same crime that his predecessor, Conrad Phelps, had been accused and convicted of. In fact, there was speculation that the reason Samson had worked so diligently to put Conrad Phelps behind bars was because he had intentions of running for office himself. It was no secret that someone was determined to bring him down.

He quickly discovered that the criminals he'd placed behind bars a few years prior had accomplices on the outside who were intent on seeking revenge. They worked diligently to destroy him—and so far, they had been successful. Although the allegations were completely unfounded, supporters began to pull their funds. And although Samson had been cleared of all misgivings, his name and reputation had already been tarnished. And all hopes of becoming mayor were gone.

He wasn't sure that returning to his old job was what he really wanted. What he really needed was to get away. Before he knew it, he'd found himself on a nonstop flight to the Eleuthera Islands. He would only return to Chicago when his head was clear, and not a day before—*if at all*.

And now, as he looked over at Alyson, who clapped her hands to the music, he wondered just how long he'd find himself in the Bahamas.

# Chapter 10

She'd spent a great deal of time searching for the perfect outfit, and she'd fussed with her hair way too long for a man that she had no interest in. She ruled out her professional garb and chose a pair of cropped white pants and a simple melon-colored blouse instead. After slipping into a pair of white leather sandals, she dabbed perfume behind each ear and in between her ample breasts.

Alyson's stomach churned as she stepped onto the beautiful terrace of the Rock House. She'd never been nervous around anyone in her life, but Samson Steel caused her anxiety for some reason. She spotted him as he took a sip of his martini. *The nerve of him, starting without me*, she thought. He stood when he saw her, greeted her and then pulled her chair out. *At least he's a gentleman*. She was startled when he kissed her cheek, but smiled a little when she caught a slight whiff of his cologne. She took a seat, and her back reclined against the wooden chair. Her gaze veered toward the beautiful sunset that was now descending upon the bay.

A candle danced in the center of their table, and Alyson tried with all her might to peel her eyes from Samson. He looked dapper in his tan, slim-fit Levi's and white T-shirt that hugged his core and revealed muscular tattooed arms. A straw Panama fedora hat rested upon his head. He had his own style, and she appreciated it.

"Very nice to see you." He smiled.

"Likewise," she said.

"I was afraid you might not show up." Samson chuckled.

"I considered it." She picked up the menu to distract herself from staring at him. "But I thought it rude to leave you sitting here alone."

"You mean like you did the other day?" he asked. "That was very noble of you."

"Why the insistence that I join you, anyway?"

"I think you're beautiful and smart. And I'd like to get to know you better. What's wrong with that?"

"There are plenty of beautiful and smart women on this island. Why me?"

"Why not you?"

"I'm not looking for a man right now."

"I never said I wanted to be your man. I just said that I want to get to know you better. A huge difference." He grinned a breathtaking grin.

She scowled at him. "What is your story? Why are you even here in the Bahamas? I've heard rumors, but I'd really like to hear from you."

She'd actually Googled him and read all about the scandal on the internet, but wanted to hear the story from the horse's mouth.

"What have you heard?" He set his drink down and peered into Alyson's eyes.

"That you were doing some shady stuff in Chicago, and now you're on the run."

"Is that so?"

"I heard that while campaigning for mayor, you accepted some bribes. It was a huge scandal, and you fled to the islands for refuge."

Samson laughed heartily, and then gave Alyson a sideways glance. "I did run for mayor. That part is true. Turns out I had some enemies in high places, and they didn't want me in office. So they fabricated a story that I was accepting bribes. There was no truth to it."

"Why would someone accuse you of doing something like that?"

"I was responsible for bringing down the former mayor, who was, in fact, engaged in bribery." Samson took a sip of his martini, and then opened his menu. "Unfortunately for me, he retaliated by having someone slander me."

"You know that running away from things is never the answer," Alyson stated. "You should always face your fears head-on."

"Facing your fears is not always that easy." Samson closed his menu and laid it on the table. "I'm having the lobster tail. What about you?"

"I can't seem to find anything on the menu that appeals to me. I never really liked this place. Maybe I'll just have a salad. I'm watching my figure anyway."

"Why don't you leave the figure-watching to me and order something worthwhile," he told her. "How about a nice steak?"

"I don't eat red meat."

"Why don't you like this place? It's upscale, and bourgeoisie—"

"Bourgeoisie like me, huh?"

"I didn't say that."

"You didn't have to." She gave a slight wave to get the server's attention. "For your information, this is not my type of place at all. When I'm on the islands, I prefer an old-fashioned Caribbean meal at my parents' house, one accompanied by conch fritters and collard greens. Not lobster tails and fancy steaks."

"Yes, ma'am?" The Caribbean waitress interrupted her rant. "Are we ready to order?"

"I'd like to start with a key lime cosmopolitan, with just a touch of cranberry and a little extra lime juice," said Alyson.

"Yes, ma'am." The woman disappeared.

"I think we have more in common than you think. Although I'm not all that familiar with Caribbean food, I do prefer an old-fashioned meal myself." Samson laughed. "Maybe I missed the mark a little with this place."

"I would think that a ladies' man such as yourself would be a bit more perceptive when it came to women."

"I was trying to impress you with a nice meal and a gorgeous view."

Alyson gave an appreciative smile, but turned her head toward the bay. "You were dead-on with the gorgeous view."

"Breathtaking, isn't it?" he said softly, relaxed in his seat. She could feel his eyes settle on her.

The server placed the cosmopolitan in front of her.

"I think I'll have the Chilean sea bass," she said, and then handed her menu to the server. Took a long swig of her cocktail.

She'd decided against the salad long before. Since he'd taken the time to try to impress her, the least she could do was eat. And she did just that, and enjoyed the simple conversation. Samson was easier to talk to than she'd ever suspected, and she found that she enjoyed his company.

"Would you like dessert?" he asked.

"Let's not push it," she said. "I really am watching my figure."

"What is this obsession with your weight?"

"There's no obsession. I'm just cautious."

"I think your body is perfect."

She did everything in her power not to blush, but she couldn't help it. She looked away to disrupt the uncomfortable moment. "It's a beautiful night."

"We should go for a walk along the beach after dinner. What d'you say?"

"Maybe another time," she said. "I have work waiting for me at the Grove."

"I understand."

She ordered another cosmopolitan, and before long she was feeling mildly tipsy. The more she talked to Samson, the less she wanted the night to end. She almost rethought his invitation to walk along the beach, but wasn't about to bring the subject up again. She was too stubborn. However, she vowed that if he asked again, she'd take him up on it. But he didn't ask. Instead, he motioned for the server to bring the check.

Fifteen minutes later, Samson delivered Alyson to the door of her suite at the Grove.

"So this is good night," he said.

"I had a lovely time." She was sincere when she said it.

She leaned her back against her door, and Samson drew closer. "Can I see you again?"

She breathed in his scent. She hoped he would kiss her; she wanted him to. He leaned in, and she rested her head against the door. She decided not to close her eyes. She wanted to be fully aware of him. His nose brushed against hers.

"Well, there you are," came an intrusive voice.

Bijou appeared out of nowhere, and Alyson rolled her eyes at the interruption.

"Hello, Bijou." Samson spoke to her.

"I've been looking all over for you. The band is setting up for rehearsal. Are you coming?"

"Of course."

Bijou stood there, as if waiting for him.

"Did you need something else?" he asked what Alyson wanted to ask.

"No. I'll be downstairs," she said, and turned to walk away. "Good evening, Miss Talbot."

"Good evening, Bijou," Alyson mumbled.

Samson turned back toward Alyson and attempted to pick up where he'd left off. Alyson placed a finger in the air and blocked his lips from finding hers again.

"Good night, Mr. Steel. Thank you for a lovely dinner." Alyson turned to unlock her door. "I need to call and check on my father."

"When will I see you again?"

"I don't know. I'll be tied up this weekend," she said as she turned to face him again. "My parents are planning a family dinner on Saturday, and I'm expected to be there."

"Oh, you mean the family dinner that I've been invited to attend?" He grinned. "Your mother invited me to break bread with your family."

"Oh, she did, did she?"

"She did indeed. And I'm glad now. I have an excuse to see you again."

She felt a sense of warmth in her heart—something she hadn't felt in some time. But just as sure as she felt it, she dismissed it. She didn't have any time or room for Samson Steel in her life. She was too busy for romance, and too focused to become attached to someone like him. She reminded herself that Jasmine's wedding was the only reason she frequented the islands, and that wouldn't change.

Even if Samson's almost-kiss did have her loins burning on the inside.

## Chapter 11

The house smelled of Bahamian macaroni and cheese, garlic chicken and fresh collard greens. Freshly baked johnnycakes rested on the kitchen table right next to her mother's famous rum cake. The conch had been chopped into small pieces and was ready to be tossed in a salad. Bahamian music played on her father's stereo in the living room, while her mother cooked and danced around the kitchen.

"Alyson, check the pigeon peas and rice for me," her mother instructed after taking a sip of her sky juice. "Jazzy, the conch is ready for you to make that conch salad. I've already fried up the fritters. We are on the ball."

"Yes, we are, Mother." Jasmine kissed her mother's cheek.

Alyson stirred the mixture with a large spoon. Of all the family dinners at the Talbot home, this one was causing her the most anxiety. The anticipation of seeing Samson again had her giddy.

"Why are you glowing?" asked Beverly Talbot. She brushed her daughter's hair with her fingertips.

"I'm not," Alyson denied, and pulled away from her mother's touch.

"You're wearing makeup." Beverly smiled. "Is that eye shadow?"

Alyson rarely wore more than an occasional lip gloss, and perhaps a little eyeliner to heighten her eyes.

"I always wear eye shadow," she lied.

Talbot women didn't need makeup. Their skin was flawless.

"I've never seen you wear it," said an instigating Jasmine, who stood nearby with a knowing grin.

"If you two don't stop...! I'm going to set the table." Alyson left the kitchen in a huff.

The sight of Edward walking through the front door gave Alyson a sense of normalcy. Took a bit of her anxiety away.

"Little sister." Edward greeted Alyson with a strong hug and a kiss to the cheek.

"It's about time you got here," she said. "I thought you were coming in yesterday."

"I spent too much time at the courthouse yesterday. I'm going for full custody of Chloe," said Edward.

"What? Why?" Alyson asked.

"Because she belongs with me."

"You can't get full custody!"

"Why not?"

"Because, number one, you don't have time to raise a kid. Which is the reason you're divorced in the first place," said Alyson. "And what makes you think a court would give you full custody instead of Savannah?"

"Whose side are you on, anyway?"

"I'm always on your side, but I know that courts typically rule in favor of the biological mother unless she's a lousy parent. Which you and I both know she's not. Savannah is a wonderful mother. And you two have the perfect coparenting relationship," Alyson said as she set embroidered place mats on the table. "What's really going on?"

"She's seeing some dude."

"So? You've dated women, too, since the divorce."

"But I don't bring anyone around Chloe. That's not a part of the deal. Not to mention I found out that he might be living in my house."

"Your house?"

"The one I still make mortgage payments on."

"Are you jealous?"

"Of course not!" Edward denied the obvious. "I'm concerned about my daughter. That's it. And Savannah broke our agreement. No one spends time with our daughter until the other party meets that person, checks him or her out and decides that it's okay."

"In what world does that happen?"

"In my damn world!" said Edward.

"Maybe you should have a conversation with Savannah about it."

"You don't think I've tried that? She told me that whomever she dates is none of my business. She got all self-righteous. Pissed me off! So I'm taking her to court. We'll see whose business it is when I sell the house and take Chloe."

Edward hadn't been divorced that long. She still remembered when his ex-wife had become fed up with his impossible schedule. He'd been too focused on his career, and not focused enough on his family. Savannah had begged him for more time and attention to his home life, and he'd refused. He hadn't anticipated that she would leave him and take his daughter away, but she'd followed through.

And when she filed for divorce, he was devastated. By the time he'd tried to change her mind, she was gone. Alyson suspected that he still loved her, yet he'd never admit it.

"You would do that to her?" Alyson asked.

"In a heartbeat."

"You're ruthless," Alyson teased.

"I'm not ruthless," Edward countered. "And enough about me. Why are you spending so much time on the island these days?"

"Well, in case you've forgotten, our sister is getting married in a few weeks. I'm helping with the wedding plans, *and* I'm the maid of honor."

"It's good you and Jazzy are spending so much time together. I'm happy about that." Edward smiled. "Where is my little sister, anyway?"

"She's in the kitchen with your mother…" Alyson raised an eyebrow. "Your very tipsy mother, I might add."

"She's been hitting the sky juice?" Edward laughed.

"Way too often lately," said Alyson.

Edward disappeared into the kitchen. Alyson continued to set the table, and when she looked up, she was staring into a pair of handsome eyes. Samson had arrived, wearing her favorite color. A red button-down shirt tightly clung to his chest, and a matching red-and-black-plaid fedora rested on his head. Following her father into the dining room, he removed the fedora and gave Alyson a wide grin.

"Sweetheart, have you met our dinner guest, Samson Steel?" her father asked.

"Yes, Daddy. We've met. He's staying at the Grove."

"She took me on a house-hunting trip recently," Samson added. "In the Abaco Islands."

"In Abaco? I see," her father said thoughtfully.

"I've been trying to get her to have dinner with me ever since, sir."

"I'm a busy person. With work and Jazzy's wedding, I have a lot going on."

"Maybe you should consider his offer, sweetheart. Even busy people need to eat." Her father took a drink from his bottle of water. "I'll grab you a beer from the kitchen, son. And let my wife know that you're here."

"I can get it myself, sir. You should probably rest."

"I've been resting all week! A man can't find a moment's peace with a houseful of women. I'm fine, really," said Paul John. "Make yourself at home."

Samson grabbed the stack of plates and began to help Alyson set the table.

"You should be ashamed of yourself. Lying to my father like that."

"You should listen to him and have dinner with me again."

"You should stay out of family business."

"Are you always this difficult with everyone or just me?" he asked thoughtfully.

"Just you." She couldn't help but smile.

Jackson walked in, a bottle of Merlot in his hand. "Well, hello, good people!"

"Jackson, my man." Samson was the first to give his friend a strong handshake.

"I see you found your way to the Talbot household. Glad you could make it." Jackson gave Samson a pat on the back, and then kissed Alyson on the cheek. "Good to see you, sis."

"Likewise," said Alyson.

"And where can I find my woman?" asked Jackson.

"Slaving in the kitchen," Alyson said, and then lit the candle in the center of the table.

Paul John returned from the kitchen with a bottle of Bahamian beer for Samson. He shook hands with Jackson. "Well, if it isn't my son-in-law-to-be. Good to see you, son."

"Good to see you doing well, sir," said Jackson. "I heard about your little...thing. You gave us all quite a scare."

"It was a small thing. Nothing to even discuss," Paul John said.

Alyson frowned at her father and gave him the evil eye. "A small thing," she mumbled.

Paul John changed the subject. "Did you finish that big renovation in Palm Beach?"

"All done. We put the finishing touches on the hardwood floors yesterday and installed new appliances and fixtures this morning...just in time for me to catch a flight here for dinner," said Jackson with pride. "I'm home for a while."

"Jazzy will be very happy to hear that," Paul John said as he handed Samson the beer.

"Happy to hear what?" asked Jasmine as she entered the room.

"That your man's home for a while," Jackson said, then grabbed Jasmine in his arms and gave her a strong squeeze. Kissed her lips as if he'd missed every single moment that he'd been apart from them.

"Let's retire to the living room, son," Paul John told Samson. "I'm sure there's a game of some sort on the telly."

Alyson felt awkward, standing there as the lovebirds continued to engage in a kiss. "Get a room," she said with a huff, and then went into the kitchen.

Beverly pulled a dish of garlic chicken out of the oven and placed it on top of the stove. "Let's get this food on the table, Alyson. Go ahead and take the johnnycakes and conch fritters out there."

Alyson grabbed the warm dishes with oven mitts and took them into the dining room.

"Let me help you with that," said Edward, who grabbed a warm dish and followed Alyson.

"Are you two still kissing? Jesus!" she exclaimed when she entered the dining room.

"Alyson, chill out," Jasmine said. "I haven't seen him in weeks."

"Jackson Conner." Edward reached for a handshake from Jackson.

Jackson stopped kissing Jasmine long enough to shake hands with his good friend and future brother-in-law. "Edward, how's it going, man?"

"Not bad, bro. Good to see you home."

"Glad to be here."

"Try to exercise some restraint," Alyson said to Jasmine. "Can't have you preggers before the wedding. It took us too long to find that dress!"

"Oh, sweetheart, you found a dress?" Jackson was surprised.

"Yes," said Jasmine. "I didn't get a chance to tell you with all that went on with Daddy the other day."

Alyson interrupted. "Yep, she found a dress—with a price tag that sent my father into cardiac arrest."

"Stop it, Alyson! I didn't even have a chance to tell him about the dress before I learned about his heart attack."

"I can't wait to see it." Jackson smiled.

"Not before the wedding, Romeo," said Alyson, while grabbing her sister by the arm. "Now come on, Jazzy. We need to get this food on the table."

The dinner conversation was light and jovial. The Talbot children were happy to have the patriarch of their family alive and doing well. His mild heart attack could've been much worse. They were also eternally grateful that Samson had been there and had selflessly spent the day at the clinic with their father.

"So I understand you attended Harvard, Samson," said Edward.

"I did."

"Strange our paths never crossed. Although your face looks familiar."

"As does yours."

"Jackson and I spent a great deal of time talking shit to one another during our days at Harvard." Edward laughed. "I'm proud to say that he's one of my best friends."

Jackson raised his beer in agreement. "Which is why he's my best man at the wedding. Did you get fitted for your tux, by the way?"

"It's on my calendar."

"Oh, my God, Edward! You haven't gone to get fitted?" Alyson interrupted. "Are you going to wait until the day before? What if alterations are needed?"

"Get off my back, woman. The bride only recently found a dress." Edward laughed, and caused the other men in the room to join him in laughter.

"What does the bride's dress have to do with you getting fitted?" asked Alyson. "We are getting down to the wire."

"I'm on it! I promise," Edward said.

Alyson shook her head at her brother.

"I've been so tied up with the wedding that I haven't had a chance to even think about Junkanoo." Jasmine tried to change the subject, lighten the mood.

"What's Junkanoo?" Samson asked.

"It's the highlight of the Christmas season!" declared Jasmine. "It's a huge street parade, with costumes, music and dancing."

"It's what dinner conversations are usually made of," added Edward.

"Only our dinner conversations have been about a wedding instead, this year," said Alyson.

"Junkanoo takes place the day after Christmas," Jasmine explained. "On Boxing Day."

"If you weren't getting married, I would be traveling to Nassau," said Alyson. "Junkanoo in Nassau is so much better. Folks all up and down Bay Street. There's really nothing like it."

"There's nothing wrong with being on the Eleuthera for Junkanoo," said Beverly. "It's just as nice."

"Mother, really? It's not the same," Alyson rebutted. "It's why Daddy used to take us to Nassau every year, for the bigger parade."

"It's certainly a sight to see," Paul John said to Samson. "And if you haven't experienced it, you certainly should… at least once."

"I can't wait to experience it." Samson took a sip of beer.

"What are Christmases like in Chicago?" Alyson asked.

"Christmas trees, music and family. And food, of course."

"Of course," Beverly agreed. "Your parents still alive and well, son?"

"Yes, ma'am. My father's a retired police officer. My mother was a housewife for many years. My father didn't want her to work outside the home. He wanted her to devote her life to raising us."

"I stayed home and raised my children, too," said Beverly. "Such a blessing to be able to do that."

"My wife will stay home and raise our children, too." Jackson grabbed Jasmine's hand and gave her a huge smile.

"Is there something we should know?" Alyson asked.

"No, Alyson. I'm just saying…when we decide to have children, I want Jasmine at home with them. Teaching them and loving them while I'm away working."

"Jasmine has a career. She has a bed-and-breakfast to run," Alyson said. "Right, Jasmine?"

"Well…I am sort of committed to the Grove. A lot needs to be done there," said Jasmine.

"But you said that you were going to scale back, and we were going to start a family right away," Jackson attempted to whisper.

"I know, baby, but I'm needed there more than ever now. And with Whitney deciding to stay in her teaching position for a little longer, it leaves me to handle things."

He lowered his voice. "But that's not what we talked about. You were going to talk to Alyson about moving back to the islands to help out for a while."

"That's not going to happen," said Alyson. "I'm already spending more time than necessary in the Bahamas, and I have no plans of moving back here anytime soon. And furthermore, what's wrong with Jasmine having a career? She loves the Grove."

"There's nothing wrong with it," said Jackson. "It's just that we talked about something different."

"Women are more than just baby makers. This is the twenty-first century. Things aren't like they were back in the day, when our mother literally sacrificed her entire life for our father."

"What are you saying, Alyson?" Beverly chimed in.

"I'm just saying that women don't have to push their own goals and careers aside for some man. Kumbaya. We've overcome."

"I think you should stop while you're ahead, young lady." Beverly Talbot pointed a fork at her daughter. "Before you say something that you don't mean."

"I'm just saying, Mother. Are you really happy with how your life turned out? Sacrificing your career as an educator to bear Daddy's children? And for what?" Alyson pushed the envelope. "Don't you ever wonder what your life would've been like had you followed your own dreams?"

"Yes. And you wouldn't be here today had I followed my own dreams, Alyson Talbot. Now let's change the subject," said Beverly. "Before we were distracted, Samson was telling us about his family."

"My mother is a fighter," Samson said. "She was diagnosed with cancer five years ago."

"I'm so sorry to hear it," said Beverly.

"It's in remission now, and she's faring very well. Her hair has grown back, and she isn't sick as much anymore." Samson smiled. "My brothers and I have started a fund in her honor. Each summer, we host a benefit concert, and the proceeds go toward research and education. It's held at one of the biggest parks in Chicago, and last year we made almost five hundred thousand dollars."

"That's wonderful!" said Beverly. "What's your mother's name, son?"

"Antionette Steel," Samson replied. "Everyone just calls her Toni."

Alyson dropped her fork. She remembered the tattoo on his arm. She felt a sense of relief that Toni was his mother and not some woman that he still had baggage with.

"On Christmas Eve, when we gather to sing Christmas carols, we will light a candle for Toni here in the Caribbean," said Beverly. "And all the other cancer survivors in the world."

Samson offered a warm smile. "Thank you. She would be so honored."

"Let's have a toast," added Edward, raising his glass of red wine. Everyone followed his lead. "To Miss Toni!"

"To Miss Toni," everyone chanted.

Alyson found herself staring at Samson for the remainder of the evening. She was impressed by his love for his mother—the commitment he had for her. She thought it must've been hard for him, with his mother being ill. She didn't know what she would do if her mother had cancer. For the second time in one week, Samson Steel had managed to impress her, and she was certainly seeing him in a different light.

He caught her staring and gave her a wink. She looked away, pretended not to see it. She wasn't sure what to do with the energy that she suddenly felt in her heart.

## Chapter 12

Bailey rested on his leg as Samson played the music. He waited for Jackson to sing the first verse of "I Want to Come Home for Christmas." The two bounced off each other as if dancing in step. Marvin Gaye would've been proud at how they brought the song to life. Beverly Talbot smiled and raised her glass in the air. The song was bittersweet and reminded her of Denny, her brave son who wasn't afraid of anything. She hoped he would make it home in time for Christmas and for Jasmine's wedding. It was the one gift that she wanted more than anything else.

Edward stuffed key lime pie into his mouth and washed it down with a glass of Port wine. The entire house was quiet and they listened as Jackson sang the words to the Christmas love song. Alyson was in awe at how precise Samson played his guitar.

Her opinion of him had changed without notice. She'd moved beyond attraction for him. Now he was tugging at her heart—a heart that had grown cold over the years. A heart that very few men had tampered with. A heart that very few people were allowed to enter. Over the years, she had become indifferent, unemotional. Emotions took too much energy, she thought. And she didn't have any energy to spare. She'd come to believe that if she hardened her heart, life would certainly be less complicated. But suddenly her heart was softening.

Moving to Miami had been the quickest way for her to alienate herself from a family that required her to love. The Talbots were family-oriented and loving. But she'd convinced herself that she wanted the opposite—that she was somehow undeserving of love. And she was doing a great job of staying away and burying herself in her work. Her career with the real estate firm had kept her extremely busy, and it seemed that her plan was working like a charm. But then the Grove was born, causing her to spend time on the islands again.

In the past, her relationship with Jasmine had been rocky. And even after they'd inherited the Grove, she told herself that she would only devote some time to getting the family's business off the ground, but she wouldn't make amends with her sister Jasmine. Their relationship had been strained for too long. Unexpectedly, though, life had again thrown her a curveball. Jasmine had somehow worked her way back into her heart, causing her to feel again. And now she was spending more time on the island than she'd expected. But even still, she'd promised herself that she would only devote herself to the details of the wedding. Just like with the Grove, planning her sister's wedding would be a job and nothing more. And as soon as Jasmine and Jackson said their vows, she'd go back to life as she knew it—busy and detached, and in Miami.

"Beautiful." Beverly clapped her hands. "Give us something else."

Jackson began to sing the words to "Silver Bells." Samson fretted the strings of his guitar, and the family sang the chorus along with Jackson—mostly off-key. Though reluctant at first, Alyson joined in with her family's Saturday evening caroling. By the time they sang the words to "This Christmas," she'd had more fun than she would ever admit to having. Edward wrapped his arms around Alyson's shoulders and gave her a kiss on the cheek. The two moved in unison to the music.

At the end of the night, Alyson found herself sharing a taxi with Samson to the water ferry. As they arrived at the Grove, there was a sense of *what do we do next* in the air, and *I'm not ready for this night to end.*

"How about that walk along the beach that you promised?" Samson suggested.

"This late?"

"The night is still young."

"Fine."

She followed him along the trail at the back of Samson Place, and down to the ocean. Samson reached for her hand, and held it tightly as they strolled along the moonlit beach. Waves crashed against the shore and played a harmonic tune. Soft Caribbean music played in the distance from the cabana. Samson moved to the music and encouraged Alyson to do the same.

"I don't dance," she said.

"Since when? I just saw you dancing at your parents' house."

Reluctantly, she swayed her hips under the sound of Beres Hammond's gentle voice. Watching her caused things to stir in Samson. He pulled her into his chest and they continued to dance. No words. He wrapped his strong arms around her waist, held her close. Soon she wrapped her arms tightly around his neck.

"The last time we were at the beach, things didn't go so well," she reminded him.

"Well, I'm hoping that this time will be different." He decided to go in for a kiss, and was glad that she didn't resist.

His lips touched hers gently, and the kiss was much sweeter than he'd imagined. His tongue found its way into her peppermint-flavored mouth. Her French-manicured fingertips danced their way across his face, caressed it. He held on to her waist. The strength of his arms made her feel safe. Wanted. Sexy. All the things she hadn't felt in a long time. Things she'd been too busy to feel.

Without a single word, he grabbed her hand and led the way back to the cabana. They stopped at the bar and Samson ordered drinks for them.

"I'll have a Kalik beer and a cosmopolitan for the lady."

She loved that he ordered for her. Though she was an independent woman, she loved that he took charge. He didn't care much about her independence. And he disregarded her attitude. Something about that turned her on. The bartender handed Samson the beer and the drink, and he carried them both inside. Alyson followed, which was something she rarely did—*follow*.

Once inside the Grove, he led the way to his room and unlocked the door, and she followed him inside. He handed her the cosmopolitan, and she took a good look around at his meticulous room, everything tucked neatly in its place. She reveled in the fact that he was clean and organized, just like her. She stepped out onto the balcony and watched as the waves from the ocean bounced against the shore.

"This room has the best view." She came back in and took a seat on the edge of his bed.

"Yes, it does. Your sister suggested it."

"Smart girl," she said. "She has more going for herself than I ever imagined. She's done wonders with this place in a very short time."

"It's a beautiful property," he agreed. "I understand that she needs help running the place. Why won't you move back here to help?"

"I made it clear to my family from the beginning. When we first learned that we'd inherited the Grove, I told them that I would not be moving back here. I have a business of my own in Miami."

"Right." He smiled. He seemed so cool and calm. "The real estate company."

"I know it doesn't seem like much right now, but I have a nice portfolio and it's growing."

"I believe you."

"The right connections would transform my company in a short time."

"And what are the right connections?"

"Commercial real estate," she said matter-of-factly. "I have a client whose father is a developer. I'd like to handle a few of his properties, or his whole portfolio if he allows me. If I can just get a meeting with him."

"Why not stick to residential properties? Seems that would be an easier market."

"It's easier and faster money, but commercial properties net more income."

"Why not just go work for a real estate firm that sells commercial properties?"

"I just walked away from one of the largest firms to start my own company," she said. "It was time. I have a degree in commercial development and finance. And I have my broker's license. I don't want to split my commissions. I know the game well enough that I should be able to do this on my own, and do it well."

"As with any new business, it takes time to build," said Samson.

"Absolutely."

"You're not afraid of much, are you, Alyson?" He sat across from her in the Georgian-style wing chair in the corner of the room.

She wanted to tell him that she was afraid of many things. Particularly him. He caused her the most anxiety.

"I'm afraid of more than you know," she said.

He stood, grabbed her hands and pulled her up from the bed. Held her tightly in his arms. "What are you afraid of, Alyson Talbot?"

*You*, she wanted to say, but resisted the urge.

"I'm afraid of failing at something that I've worked so hard for." It was partly the truth.

"Sometimes failing is not completely bad. Especially if you learn something from it."

"What have you learned from failing?" she asked.

"I've learned that you can always reinvent yourself. I was shamed by the scandal that went on in Chicago with the campaign. But here I am in the Bahamas, and no one knows anything about what I've endured in my past. And nobody cares."

"So you're planning on hiding out in the Bahamas forever?"

"I'm not hiding out, but I'm planning to stay here until I get my head together, figure out my next move."

"Will you run for a political office again?"

"I doubt it. But I would go back to the DA's office. That is an option. Or maybe I'll stay around here for a while."

"Why aren't you married with children?"

"You sound just like my mother. She's always asking me that."

"It's a valid question. Especially for a man who's not getting any younger," she said. "What are you afraid of?"

"Marrying someone I don't love. And besides, I haven't had one single prospect in my entire life."

"Maybe it's because you love yourself too much."

He gave her a sideways glance. "I'm just confident. I have my flaws."

Thoughts of him had interrupted her sleep since the night after their almost-kiss and invaded her mind the entire next day. As much as she wanted to find something wrong with him or his flaws, as he put it, she couldn't think of a single thing. The truth was, she admired his confidence and his heart, and she wanted to be near him.

He removed his shirt, climbed into the bed and invited her to join him. She didn't know why she obliged, but found herself climbing into bed with him. He wrapped his arms tightly around her. His lips touched hers, and his tongue danced inside her mouth. His fingertips danced against her tender breasts.

He raised himself up on one elbow and looked at her. "You're beautiful."

"You're beautiful," she said back.

His head relaxed against the pillow, and hers hit the pillow next to his. They both stared at the ceiling. He grabbed her hand, intertwined his fingers with hers. Kissed her fingertips. He grabbed his cell phone from his pocket, searching for something.

"I don't have anything Caribbean on my playlist," he said.

"Let's hear what you have."

The music permeated the small room.

"Who is it?"

"Her name is Amel Larrieux."

Alyson grabbed his phone and looked at the photo of the female artist whose voice bounced against the walls. "Is she French?"

"She's from Philly." Samson laughed. "But I think she might have some French roots. I call her my modern-day Ella Fitzgerald."

A puzzled look on her face, Alyson asked, "Ella Fitzgerald?"

"Never mind," Samson said with a laugh.

"She has a beautiful voice," said Alyson as she moved her head to rest on Samson's chest. She breathed in his scent, closed her eyes and couldn't think of a single place she'd rather have been. "You know a lot about music."

"It's my first love."

"Not law or politics?"

"Nope. They play second fiddle to my music."

"You're a wonderful guitarist," she said. "Why haven't you pursued a real career?"

"I don't want to be a starving artist. Gotta pay the bills," said Samson. "Besides, I don't think my father would appreciate me squandering my education to pursue a music career. He already has a problem with the career that I chose."

"You spent the evening with my family," she said. "Tell me about yours."

"I'm from a family of cops. My father, grandfather, my brothers."

"So you were the rebellious one."

"I've always been one to dance to a different beat. Needless to say, my father didn't appreciate that. I was supposed to be a cop, in his opinion," said Samson. "He's a rigid man. It's his way, or he doesn't endorse it."

"What about your mother?"

"She's a saint." He laughed. "But only if you don't piss her off. Then she's hell on wheels. She's strong, a fighter. She's a lot like you. She doesn't take much shit. She would like you."

"You think so?" Alyson was flattered.

"I think so." He raised himself up onto his elbow again. "Even as difficult as you are."

"I'm not difficult!"

"You are, and you know it," said Samson, "but it's who you are, so I don't mind it. You amuse me."

"Well, I'm glad that you find me so amusing."

"Not in a negative way." Samson smiled. "I love that you're true to yourself. No guessing about where you stand."

"I guess not," Alyson admitted.

As neo soul music serenaded the couple, Alyson's eyes became heavy. Before long she'd succumbed to a peaceful sleep.

Samson kissed her forehead, turned off the lamp on the nightstand and closed his eyes, as well.

## Chapter 13

The sunlight crept across Alyson's sleeping face. She squinted when she opened her eyes and tried to remember where she was. She was startled to find Samson lying next to her, light snores escaping from his mouth as he slept. She took in the beauty of his gentle face and muscular chest. He slept peacefully, and she wondered what his dreams were made of. She slipped from the bed and found her shoes, grabbed them. She eased the door open and crept out of it, pulling it shut as quietly as she could.

"Good morning, Miss Talbot."

She locked eyes with Bijou, who was carrying a plate filled with fresh fruit and a cup of steaming hot coffee.

"Good morning," said Alyson.

"Did you rest well?" Bijou asked, a questioning look on her face.

"I did indeed." Alyson took the opportunity to grin slyly, and then sashayed down the hallway to her own room.

* * *

Church was a requirement for any member of the Talbot family who found themselves on the island on any given Sunday morning. Alyson didn't argue with tradition, even though she hated attending her family's small church. She preferred her megachurch in Miami, where the air-conditioning blew heavily and the wooden floors didn't creak when you tried to tiptoe in late. Luckily she was a prompt person and didn't have to worry about the entire church turning to see when she walked in.

She slid into the pew next to her mother.

"I tried calling your room last night," said Beverly. "And your cell phone."

"I was so exhausted. Went straight to sleep," Alyson said, and then quickly changed the subject. "Where's Jazzy and Jackson?"

"En route. You know they're always late," said Beverly. "Pastor Johnson wants to have a word with them after church. About the wedding ceremony."

"Of course. I need to have a word with *him*, actually. I want to make sure he knows when and where he should be on that day."

"I'm sure that Pastor Johnson has performed many marriage ceremonies. He doesn't need you to give him instructions."

"Actually, he does, Mother. I want this day to go as smoothly as possible, from the time they walk down the aisle to the moment they dance at the reception. This family will not be embarrassed."

Beverly Talbot shook her head.

"What are you yapping about?" Edward asked as he slid in next to Alyson.

"Your sister's wedding that I've put a great deal of time

and effort into. I've spent way too much time in the Bahamas putting this thing together."

"Maybe you can go home this week. I spoke with Whitney this morning, and she'll be here tomorrow. Her school is on Thanksgiving break, and she's coming in on an evening flight."

"Whitney's coming?" Their mother smiled. "I miss her."

Alyson always thought that Whitney was their mother's favorite. Their mother always wanted to be a teacher, and Whitney was living her dream.

"So maybe you can fly back to Florida with me on Tuesday," said Edward.

"Maybe so," Alyson agreed.

The truth was, she hadn't contemplated leaving so soon.

When the choir began their rendition of "Jesus Be a Fence," their discussions ceased. She could hear the loud stamping of feet on the old hardwoods, and everyone clapped to the music, while Alyson tried to catch some air by fanning herself with her program. When her cell phone rang loudly, she frantically searched for it in her purse. Her mother frowned. She silenced it and then checked the screen to see who was calling. Samson. Alyson smiled inside. She felt guilty about basking in the thought of his strong arms wrapped around her for the entire night. She wanted to feel them again.

Jackson and Jasmine finally slid into the pew behind them, and started clapping as if they'd been there all along.

"You're late," Alyson whispered.

"We know."

Alyson had every intention of speaking with Pastor Johnson after the service, but she was distracted by the sudden need to return to the Grove. She kissed the cheeks of her mother and sister and thought of an excuse to get away.

"Aren't you coming for dinner?" her mother asked.

"I've got to get back to the Grove. Need to make some phone calls and reply to some emails."

"Are you flying out with me on Tuesday?" Edward asked. "You want me to have my assistant book you a ticket?"

"No, I'll have Jules book me a flight," she said. "I might stay until Wednesday. I'm meeting a client on Tuesday."

Edward gave her a sideways glance. He and Alyson had been two peas in a pod since the cradle. She was closer to him than any of her siblings. They swapped secrets for as long as she could remember, and he knew her better than anyone.

"Okay, whatever," he said, but gave her a look that said "something's up."

"I'll catch up with y'all later. I'll try to make it back to Governor's Harbor later this evening. Save me some mac and cheese."

She slipped into the backseat of a taxi before anyone could ask another question. At the Grove, she found Samson on the back patio, sipping on a Kalik beer and watching a Bahamas football game on the television above the bar. She slipped onto a bar stool next to him and ordered a glass of white wine.

He glanced her way. "You left without saying goodbye this morning."

"You were sleeping and I didn't want to wake you."

"Where did you go?"

"Church." She smiled. "Why? Did you want to go?"

"I might have. I could use a little prayer, too, you know."

"I prayed for you," she said. *And thought about you all through service.*

"I enjoyed spending time with you last night. You think we can do something like that again?" he asked.

"What did you have in mind?"

"Maybe dinner and a romantic stroll along the beach, and anything else your heart desires."

"Dinner would be nice. I haven't eaten," she said. "I'll have Raquel put something together."

She was glad that she'd passed on Sunday dinner with her family, because sharing conch fritters and fried fish on the beach with Samson was much more fun. She stretched her legs along the beach towel and fed Samson the last bite of her fish. Her finger lingered in his mouth as he savored the taste of it.

"That was the best piece of fish I've ever eaten."

"Don't say I never gave you anything," she flirted.

"I won't."

In her room, she shut the blinds and lit a few candles. Searched for a Caribbean playlist on her phone. Tarrus Riley serenaded them as she rested in Samson's arms—those arms that she couldn't seem to get out of her mind the entire day. His lips found hers and kissed them with passion.

He reached beneath her silk blouse and loosened the hooks of her bra, pulled the blouse over her head. Her breasts sprang free, and he gently stroked them. She carefully unbuttoned his shirt and stared at his brown, muscular chest. His lips found their way to her breasts, nibbling on each one. Soon his mouth consumed one entire breast, and Alyson moaned and closed her eyes.

He led her to the bed. She lay on her back and waited for him to finish what he'd started. He removed his trousers, and tight boxers hugged his groin and strong legs. He hovered over her and slowly found her lips again. When he lowered his body onto hers, she could feel the hardness of him against her stomach.

Before unbuttoning her pants, Samson looked at her for approval. "You okay?" he whispered.

Her nod affirmed that she was enjoying him. He removed her pants swiftly, and she felt a gentle breeze rush across her bare legs. His fingertips danced between her thighs and caused her to moan. He removed her panties and then kissed her inner thighs, one after the other. A trail of kisses led to her sweet spot where his tongue began to dance. She moved her hips to his rhythm. She was captivated by him.

He moved to the area just above her waist and planted kisses there. His tongue lingered around her navel and then worked its way back up to her breasts, and again to her wanting mouth. She touched his hardness, caressed him there.

"I want you," he whispered.

She couldn't remember the last time someone *wanted* her, but it felt good. When he removed his boxers, her breathing changed. It was all so surreal, but she found herself wanting him, too. She hoped he wouldn't be disappointed.

"You're so damn sexy." The words were wet against her earlobe. He quieted her fears with his affirmation.

She needed to be esteemed. When he produced a condom and then entered her, she moaned. Hugged him tighter. They moved to the rhythm of the music, made sweet love beneath the candlelight.

After he collapsed on top of her, she stroked his bearded face—planted little kisses across his forehead and nose. He rolled over onto his back, pulled her close. She rested her head against his chest as he gently caressed her shoulder and arm.

# Chapter 14

Alyson was officially distracted by Samson. She had completely forgotten to have Jules book her a flight back to Miami. In fact, Miami was the last place she wanted to be. She was perfectly content being on the island. She held on to Bailey. The base of the guitar rested on her thigh, and the neck was facing up. Samson's hands held on to hers, making sure they were in the right place.

"Now balance the neck between your thumb and forefinger," he said. "Back straight, love."

"Like this?" She stiffened her back and sat straight up.

"Relax a little."

She began to strum the strings of the guitar, in no particular rhythm. "I should probably just leave this to the professional."

"No, you can do this."

He showed her the basics. She began playing the major chords. Soon she was playing "Sweet Home Alabama" and singing along. Samson joined in on the verse, and the two made a spectacle of themselves as a crowd gathered in the Grand Room.

She stood and handed the guitar to him, and applause filled the room.

"Please stop." She laughed.

"She's being modest," Samson said as he took a seat on the stool.

"Bravo!" Kosmo clapped his hands with a grin.

Samson grabbed Alyson's hand.

"Stand right here," he said. "The guys in the band taught me this one."

She stood close as he began to strum the guitar and sing the words to Jah Cure's "Only You." It was a song that Alyson had heard a million times, but she had never expected anyone to sing the words to her, describing her as an offer that couldn't be declined, and sunshine in the rain. Though she tried to mask it, she was choking with emotion.

Samson wasn't the best vocalist, but Alyson found his performance admirable and sweet. She swayed her hips to the music. When he was done, the guests applauded.

Jasmine worked her way through the crowd and found her sister. "Okay, what was that about?"

"What?" Alyson could barely contain her smile.

Jasmine grabbed her sister by the arm and pulled her aside. "Oh. My. God."

"Jazzy, what is your problem?"

"You like him!"

"He's okay," Alyson stated, but was barely convincing. "I appreciate how he took care of Daddy. That's all."

"No, it's more. You're all giddy and he's singing love songs."

"He was singing for the crowd!"

"He was singing to you!"

"Okay, he was singing to me. So what?"

"Nothing." Jasmine smiled. "I just think it's sweet."

"Let's go, babe." Samson interrupted the rendezvous between the sisters, grabbed Alyson's hand in his. "Sorry to interrupt, Jasmine. But we have a sunset to catch."

"Babe?" asked Jasmine.

"I'll talk to you later, Jazzy." Alyson followed Samson toward the cabana at the back of the house.

"We're not done, missy! Your sister Whitney is here on the island. Her flight got in last night. She's been looking for you. You should come by the house and at least say hello. After all, she's your sister..." Jasmine stretched out the word *sister*, as if it were the last word of a song. "And what happened to your flight back to Miami this morning?"

"I missed it!" Alyson yelled.

Alyson followed Samson along the trail on the backside of the Clydesdale until they reached the ocean. Samson took a seat in the sand and invited her to join him on the ground.

"I'll get my pants dirty," she said.

"This isn't the time for prim and proper."

"These are Armani pants," she complained. "End of season last year, but Armani nonetheless."

"I'll pay for your dry cleaning."

"That's beside the point," said Alyson.

"Remind me to buy you a pair of trousers from Walmart. They don't have a Walmart on the island, huh?"

Alyson shook her head as she cautiously took a seat next to Samson in the sand.

"Do you even know what Walmart is?"

"Of course I do. They have them all over Miami." Alyson laughed.

"Good. The next time we're in Miami, we'll visit one."

"The next time *we're* in Miami?" Alyson asked.

"You need to go home soon, right? Don't you have appointments?"

"I do," she said. "But it's Thanksgiving in a couple of days. I've never spent one Thanksgiving without my family."

"Can you miss it this year?"

"I don't see why not," she said, but wasn't so sure how her family would feel about her absence at the dinner table. And suddenly, she didn't care.

"Okay, then. We're going to Miami," said Samson.

Alyson didn't respond, just turned her head away from Samson and smiled at the thought.

She watched the sun as it began to set, but her thoughts were a million miles away. She couldn't stop thinking about how Samson made her feel. Whatever it was they were doing, she didn't want it to end anytime soon.

Miami was a beautiful seventy-five degrees in November. Coconut Grove's CocoWalk was bustling with shoppers. Samson and Alyson strolled hand in hand along the beautiful brick patio lined with tall palm trees, high-end boutiques and bistro cafés.

"This is where you do your Christmas shopping?" Samson asked.

"Some of it. I like to pick up nice perfume and scarves for my mother and sisters. Things they can't get on the island," Alyson explained. "And I need to find a nice wedding gift for Jasmine and Jackson."

Samson wrapped his arm around Alyson's shoulder. "I don't care where we go. I just want to be near you."

She rested her head on his chest for a moment.

They stopped to listen as a live jazz band serenaded the crowd. Samson wrapped his strong arms around Alyson's shoulders as the two swayed to the music. She relaxed in his embrace, and Samson leaned down and planted a sensual kiss against her neck.

On the way back to Alyson's condo, they stopped for a café con leche at a little café tucked away on the nontouristy side of South Beach. At Las Olas Café they stepped up to the outside take-out window and ordered cups of predawn café cubanos. They took a seat on the shaded patio, and Samson was grateful for the reprieve. Christmas shopping with Alyson had been exhausting.

"So how long do you think you'll be on the island before you head back to Chicago?" Alyson asked out of the blue.

"Actually, I've been in touch with some old business contacts, and I'm strongly considering politics again."

"Seriously?" she asked. "I thought you'd never consider that again. I thought that's why you were on the island in the first place...because it had been such a horrible experience."

"It was a horrible experience. But someone very dear to me told me that I shouldn't run from my fears. I should face them."

Alyson smiled and took a sip of her café con leche. "Glad you listened."

"I guess you could say I've been inspired to not give up on the things that I really want."

"If you let a little opposition stop you from achieving your dreams, you'll never achieve anything."

"You're right. I watch you, and how dedicated you are to Alyson Talbot and Associates, and I admire your work ethic, your tenacity," he said. "I have to start building my team and planning for the next campaign. I can run for city council in two years, but I have to start now."

"Sounds like you have a plan."

"I have a little something. So after the holidays, I'm going back."

She changed the subject. "Let's go out tonight. Catch some nightlife."

"Are you serious? After you dragged me all over the state of Florida shopping for Christmas gifts?"

"The state of Florida? That's a bit of an exaggeration."

"Okay, the city of Miami, then."

"I say we get dressed up and catch a party on South Beach."

"I'm in."

Alyson wore a tight black bodycon dress, one with artfully placed lace panels. It flattered every last curve on her body. With Samson in a pair of designer skinny jeans, a white T-shirt and a charcoal-colored blazer with the sleeves rolled up, they were a handsome pair. And Samson found it difficult to peel his eyes from Alyson's curves as she sashayed around the kitchen, pretending to tidy things up before they left for their night on the town.

"Are we ready?" she asked.

"Damn, you look good." He completely ignored her question.

She blushed, and then shut the miniblinds over the sink. "Thanks."

"You're making it really hard to go out. I can think of a million things we can do right here." He grabbed her by the waist as she attempted to walk past him.

"Those are things we can do when we return. But for now, let's go have fun."

He smiled and released her. Followed her to the door. He grabbed the keys from her hand and locked the door behind them. He grabbed her hand as they entered the dimly lit parking garage. He knew she'd been to the garage by herself a million times before, but he still felt the need to protect her. He opened her car door and allowed her to step inside.

He found a nice jazz station on her stereo and then maneuvered the car toward the interstate.

"You sure you don't want me to drive?" she asked.

"I can drive. You just lead the way."

The music was loud as they stepped into the South Beach nightclub. Women were dressed in tighter dresses than the one that Alyson wore, but he thought she was by far the most beautiful.

He grabbed her hand and led the way to the bar. Wrapped his arms tightly around her as if they were the only two people in the room.

"I'll have a Heineken, and a cosmopolitan for the lady," he told the bartender, but then asked, "Are you in the mood for a cosmopolitan tonight, or did you want something else?"

"Cosmopolitan's fine."

They turned to look at the crowd. People crowded the dance floor, and all the tables were filled. There was standing room only. One seat opened at the bar, and Samson ushered Alyson there and pulled the bar stool out for her. She took a seat, while he stood close behind. The bartender placed their drinks in front of them, and she swiveled around so that she was facing Samson. He grabbed his beer, took the lime from it, sucked on it and then gave Alyson a lime-filled kiss on the lips.

"You are the most beautiful woman in here," he said in her ear, trying to speak over the loud music.

She crossed her legs and sipped on her drink. "I hope that at some point we're going to dance."

"We will. As soon as I get back from the men's room," said Samson. "Will you be okay until I get back?"

"I'll be fine."

"I'll be quick," Samson said, and then walked away.

* * *

After Samson left, the man at the bar next to Alyson gave her a smile and then leaned toward her. "What a beautiful accent you have," he said.

"Thank you." She barely looked his way. It was a compliment that she received often.

"Where are you from?"

She caught a whiff of his alcohol-filled breath. "Bahamas."

"I knew it was one of them... Jamaica, Bahamas or something," he said. "Is that your man with you?"

It was a question she hadn't pondered, but knew that she needed to provide an answer, even if it meant lying to keep Drunk Man at bay.

"Yes," she said emphatically.

"Corny ass dude. You need a real man. A man that knows what to do with all that damn junk in your trunk." He smiled and touched her rear end.

"Hey!" she yelled over the music, appalled. "Don't touch my ass again."

"You mean like this." He touched her again, and she slid from the bar stool.

He grabbed her arm. "I was just teasing. Where are you going so soon?"

She tried pulling away from his grasp.

"Let her go," Samson said as he approached the bar.

"Or what?" Drunk Man asked.

Samson grabbed him by the collar. "Or I'll take your ass outside."

Samson hadn't had to *take anyone outside* in some time, but being from Chi-Town, he wasn't afraid to do just that. The man released Alyson's hand and gave Samson a hard shove.

"Don't even waste your time," Alyson said as she stood between the two and pulled Samson away. "You have too much to lose."

Bystanders began to look their way.

Drunk man said, "I was only complimenting your woman's accent. And with a beautiful mouth like that, I bet she could suck—"

Before he finished his sentence, Samson had landed a right hook to his face. Alyson let out a loud shriek, and Drunk Man wiped blood from the corner of his mouth with a grin followed by laughter. Within a moment, a large man had grabbed Samson by his armpits and began to escort him toward the door.

"Let's go, buddy!" the bouncer said.

"I'm going." Samson pulled away, straightening his clothes. He grabbed Alyson by the hand, and the two left the club in a hurry.

He handed the valet his ticket and then turned to Alyson.

"I'm sorry." He'd blown it. He'd let his anger get the best of him, something that he rarely did. He was always in control, but he'd lost it in front of the woman who was slowly capturing his heart.

"It's okay." She gave him a warm smile and tried to make light of the situation. "Hopefully no one recognized you and Tweeted it."

"Hopefully," he said drily.

He was disappointed in himself. Spent the entire drive home rethinking things—wondering how he could've handled the situation better, wishing he had the opportunity again. He would do things differently. He was an upstanding man, a man of honor, and had never been thrown from a nightclub before.

When they got back to the condo, Samson lay down on

the leather sofa in the living room and turned the television to ESPN, while Alyson disappeared into the master bedroom, and returned shortly with a wet washcloth. She grabbed his hand and wiped dried blood away from his knuckles with the wet cloth, then gently kissed his knuckles. She got up and walked over to the stereo, turned on some music and finally grabbed the remote control from Samson, muting the television.

"You owe me a dance," she said.

His head bounced against the leather sofa, a half grin on his face.

"Come on," she demanded, and pulled him up from the sofa.

He stood and grabbed her waist. She wrapped her arms around his neck. They moved to the music.

"So you're not mad at me for making a fool of myself?" he asked.

"No," she said simply. "I can't remember a man ever making a fool of himself for me."

"I lost it. It made me crazy hearing someone disrespect you like that," he said. "I'm sorry I ruined your night."

"The night is still young." She stood on her tippy toes and kissed his lips. "And not at all ruined."

He held her tighter and plunged his tongue into her mouth. Grabbed the roundness of her behind. He'd wanted to do that since he first saw her in that dress. He was falling for her, and she him. And neither of them knew what to do about it.

## Chapter 15

She opened the white envelope with the red-and-gold monogrammed seal. It was a formal invitation with raised lettering, and a personal note inside.

Alyson,
I hope you can make it.
   This is a great opportunity for you to meet my dad.
   Pick his brain.
   And bring that handsome man you've been seen gallivanting about town with. The sexy one...
Best wishes,
Jennifer Madison

She quickly slipped the note back into the envelope and placed the invitation on the table.

"What's that?" asked Jasmine.

"Invitation to a fundraiser hosted by a client. It's next weekend on Abaco."

"You're not going," said Jasmine. "You can't."

"I am going. I have to. This is about my career."

"We're down to the wire with these wedding plans. Have to make sure everything is right. The caterers, the band, the men getting fitted for their tuxedoes. Christmas is less than a month away. And have you even gone to the final fitting for your dress?"

"Of course…" Alyson lied, but then dropped her head. "No. But I will. This week, I promise."

"Alyson! What is going on?"

"Nothing."

"There was a problem with Whitney's dress, and the seamstress wasn't sure if she could have it altered in time." Jasmine placed her hand over her face and sighed. "I've been looking for you all this week! Where were you?"

"I had to fly back home to Miami. Had business there. I told you I have to split my time between the islands and Florida. My business doesn't stop because you're getting married, Jazzy. My work is priority."

"I know that, but can you let us know when you're going away? The people who love you also worry about you."

"I'm sorry. I should've said something."

"Yes, you should have. Instead, I have to see it on Twitter."

"What?"

Jasmine handed Alyson her phone. There was a photo of Samson punching Drunk Man in the face. The caption read Washed up Illinois mayoral candidate takes his frustrations out on an innocent bystander. #SamsonSteel #MiamiHeat

"What the hell?"

"My sentiments exactly. Imagine my shock when I saw

your face in the background," said Jasmine. "Now again I ask, what is going on?"

"Oh, my God. Samson is going to freak. It was just one big misunderstanding. He was defending me against that creep, and the story got twisted."

"As if he needs any more trouble," said Jasmine.

"It wasn't his fault," Alyson defended him.

"I was just surprised to see you and Samson…in South Beach…together…"

"I know it seems strange, but…"

"Are you sleeping with him, Alyson?"

"Well…"

"You are!" Jasmine exclaimed. "When did this relationship go from dinner at the Rock House to a weekend rendezvous in Miami? Did he stay at your condo?"

"Eat your breakfast, Jazzy," Alyson said, hoping to avoid any further conversation about her love life.

"I want to know every single little nasty detail. And don't leave anything out," Jasmine said.

Their sister Whitney walked up, saving the day.

"Well, if it isn't my elusive big sister," she said.

Alyson stood and gave Whitney a tight squeeze. "Good to see you. Missed you!"

"I can't really tell, honey, because I've been on this island all week, and this is my first time seeing you." Whitney took a seat at the table. "Did you completely forget about Thanksgiving dinner?"

"I'm sorry. I've had business in Miami." Alyson glanced at Jasmine, who raised her eyebrows.

"I understand you have a little business here, too." Whitney grinned. "I've heard rumors about a certain tall glass of water."

Alyson peered at Jasmine, who gave her a look of guilt.

"It's not like you're hiding it," Jasmine defended herself. "And besides, social media tells all your business."

"I'm happy for you," said Whitney. "Glad to see you've finally moved past that Jimmy Franklin thing."

An uncomfortable silence filled their space. Jimmy Franklin had been a sore spot for Alyson and her family.

"Sorry, I didn't mean to open old wounds," Whitney said. "It's just that you and Jazzy lost so much time over that whole thing."

"But we're over it now. After Jazzy told me what really happened."

Jimmy Franklin had been Alyson's high school sweetheart, until he was sent away to Philadelphia. For years, Alyson didn't know why he'd been sent away—only that Jasmine was responsible. Only recently had she learned that all those years ago, Jimmy Franklin had tried to rape Jasmine. The revelation had been the beginning of healing old wounds for the sisters.

"I'm just glad to have both of my sisters back," said Whitney. "And I'm excited about Jazzy's Christmas wedding! Give me all the details of what to expect."

"The rehearsal dinner is scheduled for Christmas Eve. We'll have a Bahamian spread, of course. Raquel is putting a menu together as we speak. The fellas are planning a bachelor party for Jackson, and of course we have some wicked things planned for Jazzy later that night."

"No strippers!" warned Jasmine. "And I mean it. I don't want some strange man shaking his stuff in front of me. I'm perfectly happy with the stuff I have at home."

The sisters laughed.

"You know that the guys are going to have a stripper."

"Jackson promised they wouldn't."

Alyson and Whitney looked at each other, and then laughed hard.

"Anyway," Alyson continued, "early Christmas morning we're having a masseuse and a hairstylist come to the Grove and pamper us and make us pretty."

"Why did you both laugh about the stripper?"

Alyson disregarded Jasmine's question and continued with her wedding itinerary. "The wedding starts promptly at noon. We will be on time. And I mean it, Jazzy. Make sure that everyone knows that this wedding will start with or without them. Groom included."

"Now, how in the world will you have a wedding without the groom?" Whitney asked.

"We'll manage it. We'll put him on speakerphone." Alyson laughed. "Immediately following the ceremony, the guests will migrate to the cabana on the back on the Clydesdale. They'll mingle and buy drinks at the cash bar while the crew rearranges the seating for the reception."

"Sounds wonderful! I'm leaving tomorrow, but will be back for Christmas break. I'll get here a few days early in case you guys need my assistance," Whitney said, her hands propped beneath her chin and a dreamy look on her face. "I'm so happy for you, Jazzy...you found your knight in shining armor. I hope to be so lucky someday."

"First you have to lose these nerdy glasses," Alyson said as she removed her sister's glasses from her face, "and you need to let your beautiful hair down. You look like a schoolteacher."

"I am a schoolteacher. And this from a woman who doesn't even understand what it means to dress down," said Whitney.

"She's been letting her hair down lately." Jasmine smiled. "Now that a certain man has her attention. Or should I say, she has his?"

"About this guy..." said Whitney thoughtfully.

"We're not having this discussion." Alyson stood. "I

have to go. I have a lot of work to do today. Breakfast was nice. I'll see you both at the house later."

Alyson kissed each of her sisters on the cheek, left the Talbot house and walked next door to Samson Place. She rushed up the stairs to Samson's room and knocked on the door. He answered, a plush white towel wrapped around his waist and a toothbrush in his mouth.

"Good morning, love," he said.

"Good morning," she said, feeling as if she'd interrupted him too early. "I'm sorry, I didn't realize you were just now moving around."

"Don't worry about it. Come on in." He opened the door wider. "What's on your mind?"

She held her phone in the air, showed him the Twitter post. "Have you seen this?"

He nodded. "My brother sent it to me last night. Damn shame how they twist details."

"You're not concerned at all?"

"No. People take things to social media all the time, and always out of context. I'm used to it."

She was relieved that the Twitter post wasn't a problem for him. She needed him calm for her next order of business.

"I wanted to ask you something."

"I'm all ears."

"I have this invitation from one of my clients. She's the owner of the magnificent home on Abaco—the one we visited not long ago."

"The mansion," he concluded with a grin, and then sarcastically said, "the one I can't afford."

"Anyway—" she ignored his quip "—the owner, Jennifer Madison, is having a fund-raiser dinner there this weekend. It's a black-tie affair…five hundred dollars a plate—"

"Five hundred dollars a plate!" he repeated.

"Don't tell me you haven't been to functions like this. You're a politician. At any rate, there will be lots of big, important people there. Namely, her father, Jonathan Madison, with whom I'm hoping to do business. He owns several commercial properties, and I think it would be prosperous for Alyson Talbot and Associates to dabble in the commercial industry."

"You mentioned that," he said, and went into the bathroom. Spit in the sink, rinsed his mouth.

"I need a date for the fund-raiser. Well, maybe not a date…an escort," she said thoughtfully. "I just need someone to accompany me."

"So you need me?" he asked, coming back into the bedroom.

"If you don't want to go…or have other plans…"

"I'd love to go."

"Really?"

"Of course," he said.

"It's black tie."

"Okay."

"They have a tuxedo rental shop on the island…" Alyson began to suggest. "I can show you where it is."

"I have a tux, for your information, Miss Presumptuous," Samson said as he grabbed a pair of boxer shorts from the chest of drawers.

Alyson grinned. "It's Saturday night at seven. I'll have Stephen drive us over in his boat."

"I look forward to it." Samson dropped his towel and slowly stepped into the boxers. "Did you need anything else?"

Alyson inhaled deeply. Took in every inch of him, from his chiseled chest to the bulge in his briefs. She needed to feel him between her thighs again, is what she needed. He was quickly becoming her addiction, making her weak. He had her out of character.

"No, I'm good," she said and headed for the door.

Samson stood in front of the door, blocking her from leaving. "You're sure?"

She needed to exercise control, preserve her dignity. She was a strong woman and wouldn't fall prey to the advances of any man. And he needed to know that just because he planted little sensual kisses up and down her neck, she wouldn't give in. And just because his mouth engulfed hers with a passionate kiss, he couldn't break her. Even as he began to gently squeeze her breasts, she was still in control.

Or so she thought.

# Chapter 16

Christmas lights adorned the magnificent property. Stately palm trees stood glamorously about the grounds, while huge wreaths and garland played peekaboo in every window. The mansion smelled of cinnamon and cranberry. Red and gold candles burned in every corner of every room. Soft Christmas jazz played faintly as trays filled with flutes of champagne traveled about.

Samson looked dazzling in his navy tuxedo. Alyson wore a matching embellished navy gown that flattered her figure. The two were a handsome couple as they arrived at the Madison property. Alyson slipped her hand into the crease of Samson's arm as he escorted her inside. They quickly began to mingle, and Samson grabbed a flute of champagne for each of them. He handed Alyson hers.

"This place has transformed since we were last here," Samson whispered.

"It's so beautiful here."

"Did I tell you how beautiful you look tonight?" he asked.

"Not once." She smiled.

"Well, you are, Miss Talbot."

"And you are very handsome, Mr. Steel."

Samson leaned into her ear. "If all these people weren't around gawking at us, I swear I would kiss you."

"Good thing you know the importance of public appearances."

"I'm only exercising self-control because of you. If it were up to me, I would pretend we were the only two people in the room."

Alyson took a sip of her champagne.

"Alyson Talbot," she heard a familiar voice say.

"Jennifer." Alyson smiled and gave her a hug. "So good to see you."

"And you, as well," said Jennifer. "And you must be Samson the Great. I've heard so much about you."

"Really?" asked Samson.

"Not really." Jennifer laughed. "Actually, my friend here has been pretty tight-lipped about you. But I'm glad she brought you tonight."

"Samson, this is Jennifer. Jennifer, Samson," said Alyson.

"It's so good to meet you." Jennifer smiled.

"Likewise," said Samson.

"I hate to steal her away so soon, but I have some important introductions to make. You understand, don't you, Samson?"

"I do, indeed," said Samson.

"Good, then. Please feel free to mingle, and do make yourself at home."

Alyson offered Samson a look of apology, as she was whisked away to talk business with Jennifer's father. A tall, handsome man with graying sideburns, Jonathan Madison had a welcoming face and appeared more approachable than she had presumed he would.

"Dad, I'd like for you to meet Alyson Talbot." Jennifer grabbed her father by the hand. "She's the one I've been telling you about. She's the listing agent for Madison House and a few of my other properties on Fisher Island."

"Ahh, Alyson." Jonathan took Alyson's hand in his and kissed the back of it. "I've heard great things about you. I understand that you secured a contract on one of my daughter's properties in a matter of days."

"I did."

"So good to finally meet you."

"You, too, sir. It's an honor."

"Police Chief Taylor just walked in. I'm going over to say hello," Jennifer said before she excused herself.

"My daughter speaks quite highly of you, Miss Talbot," said Jonathan. "I understand that you used to work for Bell, Armstrong and Glenn. One of the best commercial real estate firms I know."

"Yes, sir. However, I've recently stepped out on my own. Started my own company."

"So I'm told," Jonathan said. "How's that working for you?"

"It's a slow grind, but I'm optimistic."

"I remember when I took that leap of faith and started my own development company. I was a youngster back then, fresh out of college. Long blond hair and an attitude as big as the world. I was invincible back then—a smartass with audacity." He laughed. "It takes a great deal of courage in this industry."

"Precisely."

"I understand you have plenty of ideas for the company, and I'd like to talk with you further." He pulled a business card out of the inside pocket of his jacket and handed it to her. "Call my office on Monday and schedule a lunch meeting with me. I'd love to hear your ideas for taking Madison Development to the next level."

"I will, sir." Alyson smiled. "I look forward to it."

Alyson shook Jonathan Madison's hand and then worked her way back over toward Samson, who was making small talk with a brunette. Alyson took note of her sexy red Antonio Berardi cocktail dress with the exposed back.

"Hey, babe," Alyson said, placing a hand on the center of Samson's back. She wanted to make the brunette aware that Samson had come with her, and he'd also be leaving with her. "What's going on?" she asked sweetly.

"Alyson, this is Miranda. Miranda, Alyson." Samson made the introductions right away.

"Good to meet you, Alyson. Sam and I were talking politics." She smiled.

*Sam*? Alyson faked a smile. "Really, Sam?"

"Yes!" Miranda went on to explain. "Turns out we have a common enemy. Conrad Phelps."

"Conrad Phelps was the crooked mayor that I told you about—the one I helped to put behind bars when I was in the DA's office," Samson explained to Alyson. "The one who was accepting bribes and misusing his power as a public official."

"Amongst other things," Miranda added. "That entire Blue Island ring should've met its demise long ago. Kudos to you for bringing Phelps to justice, Sam." She grinned and moved closer into Samson's personal space. "Too bad those Blue Island scumbags got off scot-free."

"Many of them are behind bars, as well," Samson said.

"Take a look around. Many of them are here tonight," said Miranda.

"What do you mean?"

"Many of the scumbags from Blue Island are at this party. Blue Island and Madison Development are one and the same."

"I don't understand," said Samson.

"It's all one big corrupt piece of work. William Blue and Jonathan Madison are old friends," said Miranda. "They're all crooks if you ask me, and should all be behind bars."

"They should be behind bars because they're old friends?" asked Alyson. "Since when did it become criminal to be affiliated with someone?"

"When the principals from one crooked company are the same as the principals of another crooked company, and are all engaged in criminal behavior. It raises an eyebrow," Miranda explained.

"I agree," said Samson.

"Half the folks in this room should be in jail if you ask me," said Miranda. "Everyone from Devin Curry, the company's CFO over there, to Jonathan Madison himself."

A tall man dressed in a charcoal-colored tuxedo worked his way over to Miranda. "Are we having a good time?" he asked casually.

"A blast!" Miranda replied.

The man grabbed Miranda by the waist, taking the champagne flute from her hand. "I think you've had a bit too much to drink."

"Honey, I'm just getting started."

"Champagne really doesn't agree with you, sweetheart. You know that," he insisted, and offered Samson and Alyson an apologetic smile.

"I haven't had that much, and I'm fine!" Miranda said.

"Let's mingle," said the tall man as he pulled her away. "Excuse us."

\* \* \*

Samson gave a nod as Miranda and the other man walked away. He was unsettled. His stomach churned.

"You know there's no merit to anything that drunk woman said," Alyson countered.

"I don't know that," said Samson.

"The Madisons are upstanding people," she whispered. "I know them."

"I know you want this business deal badly, Alyson. But I caution you to proceed carefully. A scandal would ruin you before you even got started."

"I'm not worried." She grabbed a champagne flute from a moving tray, took a drink. "Let's step outside for a bit. You look like you could use some fresh air."

They stepped out onto the veranda, and into the moonlit night. Samson's mind raced as he looked around at the guests now, trying to put names with faces. He wondered how many of them had been affiliated with Blue Island. Alyson touched his chest with the palm of her hand.

"Relax, baby. You're too preoccupied." She snuggled up to him.

"We should go," he said. "Can't we have Stephen come back for us?"

"We haven't even had dinner, silly. And need I remind you that we paid a pretty penny for these plates?" She giggled. "And besides, we decided to stay on Abaco for the night. Remember? Stephen is halfway back to Harbour Island by now. He won't be back until tomorrow. And we have a room booked at a wonderful resort just a few miles from here."

"You're right." Samson caressed her face with his fingertips and then planted a kiss on her lips.

"Don't forget our plans. We're going to stay up all night, doing God only knows what…" He was shocked at how brazen she was. "And then we're going to sleep late in the morning. Have breakfast in bed. And then do those same things all over again."

Samson conceded. He'd never seen her like this, with her guard down. He wanted to take her to that room before she came to her senses, or sobered up. It was clear that, like Miranda, she'd had way too much champagne. His mind raced a mile a minute, and as much as he wanted to spend a romantic night with the woman who'd hijacked his heart, the truth was, he couldn't wait to get to a computer to research everything that Miranda had said.

He survived dinner, even while speculating that he was breaking bread with criminals—and not just any criminals, but ones that had cost him his career. They were dressed in tuxedos and after-five dresses and pretending to be concerned about a worthy cause. They hid behind their checkbooks and hefty bank accounts. But he knew that as soon as Monday morning arrived, they'd go back to engaging in their shady business deals.

He cut into his juicy fillet, and the steak melted in his mouth. He smiled as he took a glance at the small portion of food on his plate—his five-hundred-dollar plate of food. He knew that before the night was over, he'd be ransacking the kitchen at the resort where they were staying and taking them for every morsel of Caribbean food they could muster. He hoped the property had as good a cook as the Grove did. Sometimes in the middle of the night, he'd sneak to the kitchen for a hearty helping of Raquel's johnnycakes and conch fritters. He hoped he could make it through the night without them.

When Samson looked up from his plate, his eyes met with a pair of familiar blue ones. The wicked smile caused an unsettling feeling in the pit of his stomach. William Blue gave Samson a wink and a wide grin. He stared at the slender blond man. Couldn't peel his eyes from him. William Blue was engaged in conversation with Jonathan Madison. The two of them laughed and toasted with glasses of brown liquor. Samson wondered how long it had been since Blue's release from prison.

"We really must go now." He stood and placed his cloth napkin on the table.

"What are you doing?" she asked. "Sit back down. I haven't even heard Jennifer's speech yet."

"I'm leaving, love. If you're with me, you have to come now."

"What is the matter with you?"

"Just trust me," he pleaded.

Alyson did just that, and it was something she hadn't done in a long time—trust a man. She followed Samson outside. She'd hoped to get Jennifer's attention, to at least say goodbye and to thank her for the invitation, but Samson's urgency prevailed.

Once in the backseat of the taxi, Samson explained his actions to Alyson. "The gentleman who was talking to Jonathan Madison...that was William Blue."

"The William Blue you put behind bars?"

"That would be him."

"Wow!" She sank into her seat. "That had to be uncomfortable for you."

"Yes, extremely."

"I'm sorry you had to endure that."

"I believe Miranda's claims are true. He and Jonathan are old friends," he said.

"Are you saying that Jonathan Madison is engaged in shady business deals?" she asked.

"I'm not saying that the Madisons are shady, but they're in bed with some pretty shady characters. And when William Blue was in prison, someone on the outside set me up. Tarnished my campaign."

"Are you suggesting that it was Jonathan Madison who set you up?"

"I'm only suggesting that they are friends. They looked pretty chummy in there to me. And it's possible that Madison is involved in some bad business practices," he stated. "And if that's the case, they are the last people I want you doing business with."

Samson's discoveries were nothing more than speculation, in Alyson's opinion. She'd already been invited to meet with some of the other principals in the coming week, and the last thing she needed was his speculations to get in the way of her closing the deal. She hated that his career was in shambles, but she refused to believe that the Madison family was somehow involved in unethical behavior.

"I have to do what's right for me," said Alyson. "I can't base my business decisions on what has occurred in your life."

As the taxi pulled up at the beachfront resort, Samson stepped out and held the door for Alyson. He grabbed her small hand and helped her climb out of the backseat.

After checking in to their lavish suite, Samson grabbed bedding from the hall closet and tossed it onto the sofa sleeper. "I'm crashing in here. You can take the bedroom."

"Are you serious right now?" she asked. "What about our romantic evening?"

"I'm kind of tired."

"Are you mad about the whole Blue Madison thing because I won't go on this witch hunt with you?"

Samson shrugged and plopped down onto the sofa. Grabbed the remote control and flipped the television on. "I have legitimate concerns."

"Okay, okay." Alyson held her hands in the air as if to surrender, then stumbled backward.

"You've had too much to drink, love. Why don't you lie down?"

He escorted her to the bedroom, lifted her in his arms and then placed her onto the bed. He removed the heels from her feet. She struggled with the zipper on her dress, and he helped her.

She wrapped her arms around his neck and pulled him onto the bed. "I want you."

"I don't want to take advantage of you."

She laughed. "Please take advantage of me!"

Samson stood, removed his jacket and loosened his bow tie. He slipped the perfectly shined Calvin Klein tuxedo oxfords from his feet and removed his pants. Tight briefs hugged his strong thighs. Alyson watched intently as he loosened every button on his shirt and tossed it onto the chair next to the bed. He slipped into the bed next to her and wrapped his strong arms around her.

Alyson fell asleep quickly. Light snores crept from her lips. Samson got up, tiptoed through the suite and turned off the television and the lights. He went into the bathroom and hopped into the shower. Tried washing his negative thoughts away, but to no avail. He replayed her words in his head: *I can't base my business decisions on what has occurred in your life.* They felt like a punch to his stomach. She wasn't grasping the scope of the situation. He was convinced that the Madisons were bad news, and he worried about Alyson's future with them. He knew he had to get through to her, but tonight he'd allow her to sleep.

He opened the bedroom's French patio doors and breathed in the sweet ocean air. He could hear the waves crashing against the shore just a few feet away. Sheer white curtains danced in the wind. Samson found some relaxing Caribbean music on his phone and settled back in bed. After meeting Alyson, he'd taken the time to download music by artists that she claimed were her favorites, and he was slowly becoming a fan of Caribbean music. He allowed Jah Cure to serenade them for the remainder of the night.

His eyes grew heavy, and sleep crept up on him. He grabbed Alyson a bit tighter and then closed his eyes. When he opened them again, his eyes met those blue ones again. William Blue stood over the bed, a wide grin on his face. He looked down at Samson and puffed on a Cuban cigar. Samson glanced at the French doors. They were closed, and one of the white curtains had been ripped from the curtain rod.

Samson's heart pounded rapidly. "What the hell are you doing here?"

"You thought I'd be gone forever, Steel?"

"You're a criminal, and criminals belong behind bars." Samson was cool and calm, and hoped that Alyson would remain asleep.

"Luckily I have friends in high places."

"You mean friends like Jonathan Madison?"

William Blue laughed. Heartily. He reached into the inside pocket of his tuxedo jacket, swiftly pulled out a silver-and-black .22 handgun and pointed it at Samson. He laughed, and his blue eyes turned bloodshot red. Then they were blue again.

Samson opened his eyes. Sat straight up. His breathing was rapid and heavy, and he wiped sweat from his face. He glanced over at the French doors. The white curtains blew in the wind, still intact—just as they were before he'd fallen asleep. When he glanced over at Alyson, she was still soundly sleeping. He relaxed, controlled his breathing.

As he slipped beneath the sheets next to Alyson, he gently kissed her forehead. He grabbed her in his arms again. Held her through the night.

# Chapter 17

The sunshine was invasive, not shy at all about shining brightly through the room. Alyson squinted as she opened her eyes.

"Good morning, sleepyhead," Samson said.

"What time is it?" she asked.

"Just past nine."

"Oh, my! I never sleep this late," Alyson said as she tried to lift her head. A sharp pain shot across her temples, and she winced. "Ooh."

"I went down and got you some coffee," he said. "How do you take it?"

"Black with two sugars." She attempted a smile. "Why didn't you wake me?"

Samson sweetened her coffee and handed the ceramic cup to her. "You needed the rest."

She sat up and took a long sip. "We should enjoy the island today. Let's grab a quick breakfast and do a little shopping."

* * *

Alyson took Samson to a hidden jewel along the beach, an authentic Caribbean restaurant with Bahamian cooks. They chatted casually while enjoying hearty plates of grits, corned beef, jack mackerel, bowls of fish stew and johnny-cakes that tasted remarkably like her mother's.

"This is definitely a different type of breakfast," Samson noted.

"This is as normal as eating eggs and bacon in North America," Alyson explained. "We always start with grits for breakfast, and add fish as our protein. And you can't have any Bahamian meal without a johnnycake."

"I've definitely had my share of johnnycakes since being in the Bahamas." Samson smiled. "However, these can't hold a candle to your mother's."

"She would kiss your face if she heard you say that. I think my parents like you. But I can't think of many people they don't like. They're a congenial bunch of people... that family of mine."

"I feel as if I've known them forever," he said. "You have a wonderful family."

"I like them most times," Alyson teased, though there was some truth to her statement.

"I get the impression that you and Jasmine haven't always been on the same page."

"When we were younger, there was a boy who lived in the next town over. I was hopelessly in love with him. His name was Jimmy Franklin." Alyson cut her mackerel croquet into fours. "Jasmine talked my father into having him sent away. And I never knew why."

"And you blamed her," he concluded.

"I hated her! For years, I hated her." The pain of the memory caused her to drop her fork. She placed her hands over her face.

"We don't have to talk about it, love."

She gave him a warm smile, and tears filled her eyes. He was so gentle with her, so accommodating. She hadn't met a man like that before.

"I don't mind talking about it. We're past it now," she explained. "One day after school, Jimmy Franklin followed her home, and...and he tried to rape her. She fought him, kicked him where it hurts and ran all the way home. She told my father what happened, and the next thing I knew, Jimmy was on a one-way flight to Philadelphia. I never saw him again after that. I blamed Jasmine for years. It was just last year that she told me what happened. The tragedy is, we lost so much time...so many years because I was stubborn."

"But things are better now, right?"

"Things are wonderful now! I have my sister back, and I've been lucky enough to be an integral part of her wedding and her life."

Samson grabbed Alyson's hands in his. He kissed her fingertips and smiled.

"So where are we going after this?" he asked.

"We aren't going anywhere until you finish all of your food." She stuffed fish and grits into her mouth.

"Yes, ma'am." He took a hearty spoonful of fish stew.

After brunch, they headed over to Marsh Harbour, which was the heart of the Abacos. Alyson explained the history of it. "It's where the majority of the island's services are located, including the post office, grocery stores and laundries. Marsh Harbour is the 'bright lights, big city' of all the Out Islands, with one traffic light."

"Plenty of boat docks and marinas," he observed.

"Yep, it's the main gateway to the other Out Islands."

Samson swung his legs as they hung over the boat dock. "The waterways are busy."

"American R & B singer Aaliyah was leaving Marsh Harbour Airport when her plane crashed," Alyson said.

"I remember that. She was filming a music video somewhere in the Bahamas. That was here, huh?"

"Right here. Such a sad time."

"Yes, it was. She was so young."

"Only proves how short life is," said Alyson. "We should enjoy every moment."

"I intend to." Samson grabbed her hand and held it tightly.

When they jetted across the turquoise waters, Alyson held on to his waist as tightly as she could. Her chin pressed against the center of his back as water splashed in her face. She loved being close to him. The Jet Ski bounced against the water, and she laughed like she'd never laughed before. She would never have been caught dead on anyone's Jet Ski before, yet suddenly Samson Steel had her doing things outside of her comfort zone.

As they reached the shore, she hopped off the Jet Ski. Wearing her one-piece bathing suit, she went for a swim while Samson returned their rented equipment. Soon he joined her in the water. She did several flips, turns, breaststrokes and backstrokes. Samson watched with a grin.

"Stop showing off," he said.

"What are you talking about?"

"Turning flips and doing backstrokes. Being a show-off."

"I'm not being a show-off. I'm a swimmer. Been one all my life." She laughed. "I grew up in the Bahamas. And I took swimming lessons."

"You're a show-off." He jumped into the water and grabbed her by the waist. His cold, wet lips gently touched hers.

"Would you like me to teach you some techniques?" she flirted.

"No! I can swim rings around you."

"Well, let's see what you got," she said.

He began to swim a backstroke and attempted to do a flip turn. She looked away as she laughed at his flip.

"So you think I'm funny?" he asked.

"No." She couldn't help but laugh.

"You think I'm funny."

He swam toward her and lifted her in his arms. She screamed as he picked her up and dunked her into the water. She wiped her face as she popped up out of the water. She splashed water at him. He, in turn, splashed her, and before long the two were engaged in a water-splashing war. Finally Samson called a truce, held his hands in the air in surrender. He invited her to jump onto his back, and he carried her to shore.

They made the short walk back to the resort. With wet, bare feet, they rushed across the hardwood floor in their suite. Samson flipped on the shower and warmed the bathroom. He stepped into the shower and beckoned for Alyson to join him.

"We don't have time to mess around. Stephen will be here to pick us up soon."

"We have to shower. Get the sand out of our cracks and crevices," Samson reasoned. "Come on. It'll only save time if we shower together."

Alyson removed her bathing suit and stepped into the shower. The warm water cascaded over her body. Samson washed her back and caressed her breasts with warm, soapy water. She closed her eyes and relished his touch. She leaned her back against his strong chest as he explored her naked body, touched her in places that had lacked attention for so long. His fingertips danced between her thighs and found her warm spot—explored it. She moaned. Her breathing increased, and she lost control.

"Just relax," he whispered and nibbled on her earlobe.

She turned to face him, began to wash his chest. She reached for his groin, caressed it as gently as she knew how. He kissed her lips with vigor.

He carried her to their bed and hovered over her. His lips kissed wet breasts and nibbled on hardened nipples. A trail of kisses was planted along her stomach, lingered at her navel. He kissed her inner thighs, and she held her breath. His tongue explored the place where his fingers had just abandoned. She curled her toes and dredged her heels into the mattress. Samson moved from her thighs and back up to her breasts. He relaxed his muscular body against hers. Pressed her legs apart, pushed himself into her. Made sweet love to her.

When her phone rang, she wished it would stop. Tried to ignore it as she moaned and buried her face in Samson's neck.

"It's probably Stephen," she finally whispered.

"I can't let you go."

"I should get it."

"Tell him to go back to Harbour Island. Let's stay another night."

"I have work this week. I need to get back to Miami," she said. "I have to schedule a meeting with Jonathan Madison."

He pressed into her one last time, collapsed on top of her and then rolled to the other side of the bed. She could tell the mention of Jonathan Madison's name annoyed him. Killed the mood for him. He stood and grabbed Alyson's phone from the nightstand, handed it to her.

"You should call Stephen back," he said.

"What's wrong?" she asked the obvious.

"Nothing," he lied.

"Oh, you thought that I wouldn't do business with Jonathan Madison because you saw him talking to your archenemy?"

"It's not just that I saw them talking, Alyson. Don't you get it? It's that there's probably more to that relationship than you know. And you shouldn't pursue this venture."

"In business we have to take risks."

"Indeed we do, love. Indeed we do." He grabbed a pair of trousers and went into the bathroom, shutting the door behind him.

On the boat ride back to Harbour Island, the atmosphere was just as cold as it had been on their first return trip from Abaco. Samson sat in the bow of the boat and never turned around to look at Alyson, who sat in the port and stared into the ocean. Stephen made small talk with Samson.

"We're expecting rain this week, and it looks like we might be getting quite a bit over the next few weeks," said Stephen. "I hope the weather is cooperative for Jazzy's wedding."

"I hope so, too," Samson said drily. The last thing he wanted to discuss was Jackson and Jasmine's impending wedding. He wanted to get through to Alyson. Shake some sense into her.

Once they reached Harbour Island, Samson and Stephen guided the boat to the deck and secured it with a rope. Samson helped Alyson climb out of the boat.

He held his hand out to Stephen. "Thanks again, man," he said.

Stephen grabbed Samson's hand in a strong shake. "Don't mention it."

"Are you bringing a date to Jasmine's wedding?" Alyson asked Stephen.

"I haven't decided yet," said Stephen.

"You should probably let us know sooner rather than later so that we can plan accordingly," Alyson said. "We haven't received your RSVP."

"I'll probably just come alone."

"What about that girl from Spanish Wells?" she asked. "The one you were all cozy with at the Grove's grand opening."

"We were just friends. And besides, she moved to Nassau," Stephen explained.

"Well, I know a nice young lady you might be interested in."

"I don't need any help in that area, Alyson. But thank you."

"She's young, beautiful…a musician," insisted Alyson. "She's in the band that we've hired for the wedding reception. Her name is Bijou."

Samson glanced at Alyson and shook his head. He couldn't believe she was actually trying to pawn Bijou off on her cousin. Anything to remove her from Samson's reach—if, in fact, he had any intentions of reaching.

"I don't need you playing matchmaker," said Stephen. "Just put me down for one."

"Are you sure you don't want to meet her?" Alyson asked.

"Positive." Stephen shook his head. "You're something else."

"I'm just trying to help."

"Handle your own affairs," said Stephen, who leaned in for a kiss to his cousin's cheek. "It seems you're not doing a very good job at it."

"I'm doing just fine, for your information," Alyson insisted.

"Really?" asked Stephen. He patted Samson on the back. "Well, let's just hope you don't run this guy away. He has an enormous amount of tolerance."

"Goodbye, Stephen." Alyson walked away from the men, pulling her cell phone out. "Thanks for the ride."

"You're quite welcome," said Stephen with a smirk. "Love you."

"Love you, too." Alyson held the phone to her ear.

Stephen turned to Samson and whispered, "She doesn't like to be challenged. Have to keep her on her toes."

"I'll remember that."

The men shook hands once more before parting ways.

Pictures were scattered about on the coffee table. Scissors and scrapbooks were on the floor. A near-empty bottle of wine was in the center of the table. Jasmine sat on the floor, her head resting against the leather chair, and Whitney laughed at something until she cried.

"What is going on?" Alyson asked her sisters.

"Well, well, well... I see we made it back from Abaco," said Whitney as she looked past Alyson and smiled at Samson. She stood and held her hand out to him. "Hello, I'm Whitney. Alyson's sister."

"A pleasure to meet you, Whitney. I'm Samson Steel."

"Yes, you are," Whitney said as she gave him a long examination.

"What is all this mess?" Alyson asked.

"We're scrapbooking. And looking for photos for the video presentation we have planned for the reception," Jasmine explained.

"We have photos of Jackson, too. His mama sent them." Whitney held a photo in the air. "Wasn't he just the cutest?"

"Adorable." Alyson was unimpressed. "And how much wine have you two had while walking down memory lane?"

"We are not drunk, if that's what you're asking," said Jasmine. "We're tipsy."

Both women giggled.

"This doesn't look good, ladies," explained Alyson. "We have guests staying here, and this just isn't a good look for the Grove."

"We're fine, Alyson. Really." Whitney changed the subject. "How was your trip?"

"It was wonderful," said Alyson.

"I'm going on up to my room," Samson whispered to Alyson. "I'll catch you later."

"You want to have dinner on the terrace tonight? I can have Raquel whip something up for us."

"Nah, I'll probably just grab a burger from Ma Ruby's later." Samson kissed Alyson's cheek.

"Okay, then. I'll chat with you later." She tried to remain upbeat in front of her sisters, but knew that something was different between them.

She watched as he climbed the stairs. Her sisters witnessed the entire exchange in silence.

"Trouble in paradise?" Whitney asked.

"No!" said Alyson. "We had a great time. He's just tired."

Jasmine and Whitney gave each other a look. Alyson took a seat in the leather chair and began to sift through the photos. She hated that the weekend hadn't ended on the best note, but she figured Samson would let things go soon. He would see that he was wrong about Jonathan Madison. He would understand that she needed to do what was best for her company.

Her business was all she had.

## Chapter 18

The Brazilian restaurant was crowded during the lunch period. With an extensive wine list and one of the best porterhouse steaks in Florida, the Capital Grille was where important business meetings were held. Alyson had chosen her best business attire—a black Ralph Lauren suit with a gray silk blouse underneath. She wanted her appearance to prove that she was capable of handling most anything—particularly Jonathan Madison's collection of commercial properties.

A young, dark-haired gentleman sat across from Jonathan at the table. Both men stood when she approached the table.

"Alyson, good to see you again. You left so abruptly the other night, I didn't get to say goodbye," said Jonathan.

"My apologies. I had an urgent matter to attend to."

"I'm glad to know that everything is all right. I'd like for you to meet Dustin Rose. He's head of finance at Madison.

He works diligently to get our buyers qualified for financing. And he has a pretty good track record."

Dustin took Alyson's hand in his. "Pleased to meet you, Miss Talbot."

"Likewise," said Alyson.

"Alyson, should we hire your company to handle our leasing and sales, you'd be working very closely with Dustin. So I thought it fitting that he join us tonight."

Alyson picked up her menu and gave it a quick glance. Her nerves had the best of her, and her appetite was barely there.

"I explained to Dustin that you've come highly recommended."

"Your credentials are impressive." Dustin smiled.

His facial expression seemed obscure, and Alyson couldn't quite read him.

"I'd like to hear your plans for our inventory in Miami, Coral Gables, Fort Lauderdale and West Palm Beach," said Jonathan. "They're close to being completely developed, and we'd like to get them on the market as soon as possible."

"I've already done a market analysis of your properties in those areas. And I've developed a marketing plan for each of them." Alyson opened her briefcase and handed Jonathan and Dustin copies of her plans. She was grateful that she'd printed an extra copy. "If you'd turn to page one, I'd like to walk you through what I have in mind."

Alyson had worked hard on her proposal. She'd done her homework and presented a well-developed plan. It was aggressive, yet realistic, and Jonathan seemed impressed with her. He knew that because her business was new, she was hungry and would put forth more effort than someone who was a veteran. She couldn't quite read Dustin's thoughts about her plan. But she didn't care. As long as she'd impressed Jonathan, it was all that mattered.

"I know that I'm being somewhat optimistic here, and this is a great deal of responsibility for a small agency such as yours..." Jonathan began.

"We're small, but capable."

"This will require your intentness. You don't have anything pressing that would distract you from this, do you?"

*You mean besides my sister's impending wedding that's scheduled to take place soon?*

"No, of course not," she said.

"I like your marketing strategy. Let's get these properties listed right away," he said. "Can we do that?"

"Absolutely," said Alyson.

"Then congratulations are in order." Jonathan smiled and reached across the table to shake Alyson's hand. "Welcome to the team."

Dustin took a long drink of his Cognac and then shook Alyson's hand. He cleared his throat. "The holidays are upon us. Christmas is right around the corner. But at Madison...we don't really have time for celebrations. Time is money, and we can't afford to waste either one," he explained. "On December 24 we have a huge company meeting at our resort in Daytona Beach."

"You mean Christmas Eve?" Alyson asked.

"Yes, Christmas Eve. While the rest of the world is drinking eggnog and Christmas caroling, we'll be talking about strategies for the upcoming year. It's how we stay ahead of our competitors," he said. "If you're a part of the Madison team, we'll expect you to be there. Right, Jonathan?"

"Well, I'm a big fan of spending the holidays with family. But I suppose if sacrifices must be made, then they just do," said Jonathan in an apologetic manner. "We'd like for you to be available during the holidays, Alyson."

"It's just that my sister is getting married on Christmas Day in the Bahamas."

"Congratulations to her," said Jonathan.

"What does that have to do with Christmas Eve, and with you?" Dustin asked.

*Besides the fact that the rehearsal dinner is on Christmas Eve, and I'm the maid of honor?*

"Nothing. I'll be there."

"The Bahamas is a short enough trip from Florida. Fly out on Christmas morning, and you'll make it just in time for the nuptials," said Jonathan.

"Absolutely."

"Jennifer told me that you're a single woman, no husband, no children. Is that correct?"

"That is correct."

Dustin smiled. "Family is a wonderful thing. But without it, you can devote more time to Madison."

Jonathan smiled. "You bring those bright ideas that you just shared, and that energy that you've shown me tonight, and we'll all make a bundle of money."

"Looking forward to it." Alyson took a sip of her wine.

Her priorities had quickly changed, and she wasn't sure how she was going to handle them.

When she returned to her condo, she opened all the blinds, unleashed the beautiful sunshine and ushered it into her space. She hit the power button on her stereo. The upbeat Caribbean rhythm bounced against the walls, and she danced. With hands raised in the air, she rotated her hips to the music. She opened a celebratory bottle of champagne, one she'd found buried in the pantry. It was a bottle that she had stashed from last New Year's Eve.

Last New Year's Eve she'd spent the holiday flipping between Carson Daly and *Dick Clark's New Year's Rockin' Eve with Ryan Seacrest* on her television set. She'd fallen asleep before midnight and never got around to popping the cork, and thankfully so. She needed the champagne now to celebrate her new partnership with Jonathan Madison.

"You should come over and have a toast with me!" she told Jules over the phone.

"I wish I could, but I'm babysitting the kiddos this afternoon," Jules said. "My sister had to work."

"Well, I'm raising my glass in a virtual toast to you," said Alyson. "Here's to us doing great things in the coming year."

"Cheers! I'm looking forward to it," said Jules. "And I want to hear all the details. But right now, I have to go before these rug rats destroy my house."

"Go!" said Alyson as she placed her glass of champagne onto the coffee table and lit a few candles. "We'll talk later."

"Let's do breakfast or lunch tomorrow and catch up."

"I'll meet you in Little Havana for breakfast."

"Oh, how I desire a café cubano!" Jules exclaimed. "Meet at Café Versailles?"

"Eight o'clock."

"I'll be there!"

"Don't be late, Jules. You know how I hate when people aren't on time."

"I'll be there," Jules assured.

"Okay, I've got to go. Someone's knocking at my door," Alyson said.

The knocker was relentless, and she was hesitant to answer. Very few people knew that she was at home in Miami. She was gone so frequently, and she did not appreciate visits that weren't prearranged. And she would let the person on the other side of her door know just how displeased she was.

After a quick peek through the peephole, she swung the door open.

"And to what do I owe this visit?" she asked.

Edward was dressed in an oxford-gray tailored suit. He always looked dapper. A precise haircut and a clean shave was his signature look. He stepped inside. "I'm really shocked that you're here. You spend so much time on the islands these days. What's that about?"

"I'm helping Jazzy with the wedding."

"And spending lots of time with that fellow, I hear. What's his name?"

"I don't know who you're talking about."

"You know who I'm talking about. Jackson's friend, the politician."

"Oh, you mean Samson." She pretended to be enlightened.

"Yes," he said. "I'm hurt that you didn't share your little love affair with me."

"Don't pout."

"Every man who has ever been interested in you, you've run away from."

"Well, there's no future here, either. He lives in Illinois, and as soon as he's done gallivanting about the Bahamas, he's going back there."

"So where does that leave you?"

"I don't know! In Miami thinking about him, I guess. Wondering what could've been. And before you say it, long-distance relationships never work. Everyone knows that. And I'm perfectly fine without the stress of a commitment."

"Sure you are." Edward smiled.

"I am!" she said, and then changed the subject. "And what are you doing here, anyway?"

"I was in the neighborhood." He picked up the bottle of champagne, held it in the air to see how much she'd drunk.

She snatched the bottle from her brother. "Palm Beach is hardly my neighborhood. What's really going on?"

Edward collapsed onto the couch and sighed. "Savannah's getting married."

"Really?" Alyson asked. "The one you don't want around Chloe because he hasn't been preapproved? And the one who's been spending too much time at the house that you're still paying a mortgage on?"

"You think I'm overreacting, don't you?"

"I think you haven't quite let go of your ex-wife."

"Things were just fine the way they were. We have such a great friendship, and we've gotten this coparenting thing down to a science. Now is not the time to switch things up for Chloe. She's finally getting it together. The divorce really messed her up."

"Kids are way more resilient than we think. They bounce back," said Alyson. "It's the grown folks who have problems coping."

"I'm over her," he tried convincing her.

"Then why is this so hard for you?"

He walked into the kitchen and rummaged through the cupboards until he found a champagne glass. He returned to the living room and filled his glass.

"I'm concerned about Chloe. I don't know anything about this guy. What if he's a sexual predator? What if he mistreats my daughter or Savannah, for that matter?"

"I don't believe that Savannah would allow anyone to mistreat Chloe," said Alyson. "But if you're so concerned, why don't you just go meet the guy?"

"I'm supposed to. This evening, actually. I'm meeting the two of them at Pascal's on Ponce for dinner."

"Ooh, Pascal's. Fancy."

"I need you to come."

"No!"

"Yes," Edward exclaimed. "I can't do this alone."

"I have tons of work to finish before I head back to the islands."

"Please, sis," Edward begged. "We won't stay for the entire meal. Just long enough for me to read his ass some rights, and share my dos and don'ts when it comes to my daughter. Now, are you coming or not?"

"Not," Alyson said emphatically. "This is none of my business, and already very awkward for *you*. Why should I suffer, too?"

"Because you love me."

"I do love you," she said.

"And because you love Chloe."

"Both very true statements," said Alyson. "But what's love got to do with anything?"

"I'll wait while you go get dressed."

"I can't go, Edward. I have a ton of work to do this afternoon, and I have an early morning with Jules. I'm hoping to be back in the Bahamas by tomorrow afternoon. You should do this alone. Get it over with."

"Yeah, you're right." He finished the glass of champagne with one gulp and set the glass on the table. Stood. Adjusted his tie.

"You can do this, big brother. And it won't be as bad as you're anticipating."

He kissed Alyson's forehead before heading for the door. "I'll call you later."

She was relieved when Edward left. The last thing she needed was to engage in someone else's drama. She had drama of her own. She knew that doing business with Jonathan Madison was a risk, particularly if Samson's intuition was right. The business arrangement was bittersweet for her—she was overjoyed to be taking her company to the next level, but the stakes were high. Besides possibly doing business with criminals, she risked losing Samson.

She couldn't wait to see his face when she returned to the Bahamas. In just a short time, he'd managed to rearrange her life and her emotions. He'd penetrated her hard exterior and made his way into her heart. She loved the way he made her feel—mentally, emotionally, physically. To imagine her life without him was painful.

She didn't know what their future held, and she didn't care. She just wanted to enjoy each breathtaking moment while it lasted.

# Chapter 19

It was important that Alyson return to the Bahamas as soon as possible. There were many loose ends that needed to be tied up before the wedding. She needed to ensure that all the bridesmaids' dresses had been altered, the grooms-men had been fitted for tuxedoes and the menu had been finalized. She needed to speak with the caterers, the cake decorators and the florist. And just as she'd promised, she needed to take her mother shopping for a dress. So many things needed to be done in such a short time. And since she'd be handling the Madison portfolio soon, she needed to help Jasmine finalize as many wedding plans as she possibly could.

Alyson's head bounced against the leather seat in first class. No need getting accustomed to flying coach, she thought, because she had a feeling she'd be flying first class from now on. With the money she was going to make soon, she wouldn't be doing anything low budget. She could continue to support her lavish lifestyle without worry. She decided to indulge in a celebratory drink. She'd gotten exactly what she wanted, and she was proud of her accomplishments.

It was midafternoon when she landed and made her way to the Grove, which was still and quiet. Most of the guests were out and about, enjoying an afternoon swim at the beach or a tour of the island. Alyson found Jasmine wandering about the Clydesdale with a notepad in her hand, her hair tousled and a permanent wrinkle in the center of her forehead. The wedding was taking its toll on the bride-to-be.

"We have a situation," said Jasmine frantically. "Daddy's tux didn't ship with the others, and it won't get here in time."

"That's an easy fix. I'm sure Daddy has a suit in his closet that he can wear."

"A silver tuxedo with a red bow tie?" Jasmine asked.

"He doesn't have to wear the same tux as the rest of the bridal party, sweetie. He's the father of the bride, not a groomsman. He can wear a regular old suit to give you away in."

"And what about Carina's dress?"

"What about Carina's dress?"

"It doesn't fit! It's too tight, and the seamstress says there's nothing more she can do about it."

Alyson shrugged. "Bottom line, Carina's got to lose weight. She has a few days to lose a few pounds, and I would suggest she get started right away. She needs to miss a few meals between now and the wedding."

"We're talking a few weeks, Alyson. I don't see her losing a few pounds before Christmas." Jasmine was near tears.

"It's doable. Bread and water diet." Alyson laughed in

an attempt to lighten her sister's mood. "Now calm down and don't be a bridezilla."

"I'm serious, Alyson. I'm stressed beyond words. I'll feel better once we get past rehearsal dinner," said Jasmine. "By the way, can you make sure Jackson's parents get from the airport to the Grove? Their flight gets in right about the time of the rehearsal dinner. Which means neither Jackson nor I can get away."

"I'll send Daddy. He can pick them up and deliver them to the Grove, safe and sound."

"Perfect," Jasmine said with a sigh of relief. "Pastor Johnson will get there at six. What time will you arrive for the dinner?"

Alyson was speechless for a moment. "Um...what time would you like for me to arrive?"

"Early," Jasmine said matter-of-factly. "We have to decorate, remember?"

"About Christmas Eve... Jazzy..." Alyson began to explain that she had a conflict.

Raquel rushed over in a panic, interrupting them. "Jasmine I really need to talk to you about the food for the rehearsal dinner. We're getting close, and I know you've been busy, but we really need to get this menu finalized."

"I know, I know." Jasmine threw her arms into the air. "What were you saying, Alyson?"

"Nothing that can't wait. Go handle the menu." Alyson shooed them along. "We'll talk later, after I get unpacked and settled in."

She was grateful for the reprieve, but knew she'd have to break the news to Jasmine at some point. She took the stairway up to her room, just long enough to drop her luggage off and take a glance in the mirror. She checked her hair and refreshed her lipstick before closing the door behind her. She almost skipped as she went next door to

Samson Place. She rushed up the stairs to Samson's room and knocked on the door. No answer.

"Where are you?" she whispered to herself.

"He's on the cabana," said Bijou as if she'd heard her. "We just had a drink together."

"Thanks." There was something about that woman that she couldn't stand, but she'd vowed to never let her know it. Instead, she killed her with a kind smile and a cool demeanor.

She found Samson on the cabana at the bar, just as Bijou had said. He was nursing a bottle of Kalik beer. His eyes were glued to the television as he watched a soccer match. She crept up behind him and wrapped her arms tightly around his waist.

"Don't you have anything better to do with your time?" she asked.

"No, nothing." He turned around, faced her with a smile and then pulled her close to him. Kissed her lips. "When did you get back?"

"Less than an hour ago."

"Good to see you," he said. "Have a seat. What would you like to drink?"

"The usual. So I understand you just had a drink with Bijou."

"Well, she was just down here at the bar. I had a drink, and she had one. If you consider that having a drink together, then I guess we did." He laughed.

"What is with her?" Alyson asked.

"She's young and infatuated with your man."

*"My man?"* Alyson leaned her head back to get a good look at him. "Is that what you are?"

"I'd like to be." He caressed her face with his fingertip and then grabbed her chin, pulled her in for a kiss.

"Deuce, give the lady a cosmopolitan," Samson said to the bartender.

"Are you new?" Alyson asked the Rastafarian with long locks that spanned the center of his back.

"Yes, ma'am," he said. "Today's my first day."

"Who hired you?" Alyson asked. "And what happened to Vick?"

"I believe your sister Jasmine hired him," Samson interjected.

"I guess I've missed some things." She sighed and climbed onto a bar stool next to Samson.

"All this back and forth between the islands and the States. It has to be exhausting," said Samson. "You miss so much."

"I won't have to go back to Miami until the week of Christmas," she said. "I have a meeting on the twenty-fourth."

"Must be an important meeting. That's Christmas Eve, in case you didn't know."

"I know."

"And isn't the rehearsal dinner on that day, as well?"

"I'll be back in time."

"Will you, Alyson?" Samson asked. "This is an important day for your sister."

"I'm going to try my best."

"Aren't you the maid of honor?"

Alyson was quiet. He already knew what her position was in the wedding. And he wasn't making this any easier. The thought of not being on the island on Christmas Eve had already caused her angst. She couldn't remember a single Christmas Eve that she hadn't spent with her family. All the Talbot children would arrive home a few days before Christmas. They'd spend time cooking, singing and dancing to Caribbean rhythms while wrapping gifts.

They drank wine and told stories until the wee hours of the morning on Christmas. It was an important time for the Talbots, even when there wasn't an impending wedding.

"Have you told Jasmine that you're going to miss her rehearsal dinner?"

"She's got so much going on… I don't know how to tell her."

"What kind of meeting is scheduled on Christmas Eve anyway? Can't it wait until after the holidays?"

"I wish it could." She took a sip of the drink that Deuce set in front of her. "But the Madisons—"

"The Madisons?" Samson interrupted. "That's who you're meeting with?"

"Yes," she said solemnly.

"So you're still planning to do business with them, despite my warnings," said Samson. He laughed sarcastically and took a long drink of his beer.

"Yes."

"You know, I did my homework. Discovered some pretty alarming things about that company."

"Really?"

"Just as I suspected, many of Blue Island's principals are the same as Madison's. And guess what else I discovered?" He didn't await her response. "Madison is up to some of the same old business practices that his buddy William Blue was. Bribing building inspectors and city officials, tampering with public records. The city's chief of development got a new SUV this year…and I can only guess whose name is on the bill of sale. I bet if I were to dig deeper, I'd find Caribbean cruises and payments of mortgages, too."

"It's all hearsay. I don't think Jonathan Madison would knowingly engage in such behavior."

"Don't be naive, Alyson. If I were the DA in that town, I'd throw the book at them!"

"Well, you're not the DA. Isn't that why you're here in the first place?" she asked and instantly regretted her words. The last thing she wanted to do was say something hurtful to Samson.

"It's only a matter of time before they're brought to justice. And when it happens, you'll be caught up in it, too," said Samson. He stood, placed two bills on the table to cover their drinks. "Consider yourself forewarned."

"So what does that mean for us?"

"There is no *us* if you're planning to do business with criminals."

"Are you asking me to choose between you and my career?"

He thought for a moment, and then brought his lips to her ear. "I guess I am."

He awaited her response.

Finally, her silence was response enough. He walked away.

She was stunned. Couldn't move. Her heart raced a million miles per minute. She wondered if there was any truth to Samson's findings, or if he was simply being paranoid. William Blue showing up at the party had him shaken, and seeing things that perhaps didn't exist. She wasn't an unethical person, but she needed more than the accusations of a former assistant DA and a washed-up politician to make her squander such an important business partnership.

Her career was dependent upon it, and no one came between her and her career. Not even Samson Steel.

# *Chapter 20*

It had been a few days since he'd spoken to her, and Samson was beginning to rethink everything he thought that Alyson Talbot was—beautiful, intelligent, brilliant, strong. At the end of that list, he thought he should add *unethical, immoral* and *calculating*. Her choice to continue to work with Madison Development would drive a wedge between them, and he knew it. He questioned whether or not he could trust her, and decided that it was better to cut ties with her sooner rather than later—before his feelings were all caught up in a woman who couldn't care less about him. She had her own agenda, and she was willing to carry it out despite the costs.

He'd come to the Bahamas to get away from his troubles in Illinois. Now it seemed that trouble had followed him there. Perhaps it was time to return home and face his fears. Jackson would understand if he missed the wedding. He lifted the suitcase onto the bed and opened it, began to fill it with his clothing. There was a struggle going on between his heart and his mind. His heart wanted to believe that he could get through this with Alyson. He'd already begun to feel things for her. But his mind had always been the more dominant force. It kept him out of predicaments.

His afternoon flight was on schedule, and he made it to the airport just in the nick of time. Dressed in a pair of khaki-colored cargo pants, a blue T-shirt and a white blazer, he stepped out of the taxicab. His pageboy hat blew from his head, and he quickly grabbed it before it took flight. He handed the driver two Bahamian bills, both with Queen Elizabeth II's face plastered across the front of it. The portrait of Hope Town, Abaco, depicted on the back of the bills reminded him of time spent with Alyson on the Abaco Islands. He enjoyed those moments with her. He would miss her gorgeous smile and her incredible body. Despite their differences, he would feel her absence.

"Keep the change," he told the driver.

The flight from the Eleuthera Islands to Chicago was long and exhausting. But he was grateful when the aircraft's wheels hit the pavement at Chicago's Midway. The brisk winters in Illinois were a far cry from winter in the Bahamas. He was grateful that he'd packed his insulated parka with the hood. He slipped his snow boots onto his feet before stepping out to the curb to hail a taxi. Large snowflakes brushed against his unshaven face. He slid into the backseat of a yellow cab.

Twenty minutes later, he stepped inside his loft on Printer's Row. The 1960s warehouse had been transformed into a trendy living space equipped with beautiful hardwoods, high ceilings and brick walls. An abundance of natural light beamed through massive windows. He tossed his keys onto the end table, headed straight for the thermostat and turned on the heat as he shivered from the cold. He plopped down onto the caramel-colored leather sofa, still bundled in his parka. A glimmer of guilt rushed over him as he looked around his contemporary loft. He'd teased Alyson about her downtown condo, while he enjoyed much of the same luxuries that she did. He'd moved from his old neighborhood years before.

After the space began to warm, he took off his coat. His kitchen was modern, with granite counters and stainless-steel appliances. His refrigerator was bare except for a two-liter bottle of flat Coke, a half-dozen eggs and a carton of milk. He frowned as he poured spoiled milk down the drain. He removed his boots from his feet and flipped on the television, tuned it to CNN to catch the latest goings-on.

Once the snow subsided, he headed out to visit his mother. Antionette Steel had short, silver hair and golden-brown skin. She looked smaller than he remembered her being just weeks ago, but then she'd always had a petite frame, even before she became ill. Even as small as she was, she was a feisty ball of fire. He loved her spunk. Chemotherapy had managed to steal her hair, but not her positive energy.

She screamed when she saw him. "What are you doing here?"

"I had to come see what mischief you were up to," he teased her and gave her a strong hug.

She grabbed his face in her hands. "So good to see you, baby. I can't believe you left the gorgeous Bahamas for this terrible weather."

"Some things you just have to do."

"What's really going on?"

"I told you. Had to come check on my favorite girl." He smiled.

"I'm fine." She pulled a pound cake from the oven. "You need to find yourself a nice girl, settle down and have some babies."

"I found a girl, but I don't think she's the right one."

"Really?" she asked. "In the Bahamas?"

"Yep." He pinched a piece of cake between his fingers and quickly stuffed it into his mouth.

Toni slapped his hand. "Are you crazy, boy? Messing up my cake! Now tell me about this girl."

"Nothing to tell. She came. She went."

"Was she pretty?"

"Gorgeous!"

"From a good family? Got good child-bearing hips?" Toni giggled.

"Ambitious, successful…" He moved his face close to her ear. "Sexy."

She waved him away. "Then what's the problem? You have too many rules and expectations, Sammy Steel."

He explained to his mother about the relationship between Alyson and Madison Development, and the man he'd sent to prison, William Blue. He told her how Alyson had refused to heed his warning.

"I don't know if I trust her," he said.

"I understand how you must feel," said Toni. "But you have to understand her position, as well. This is her livelihood, and she can't be expected to put her life on hold for a man she barely knows."

"I don't want her to be cautious for me. I want her to be cautious for her own good."

"You sound so protective." She brushed her hand across her son's face and then said emphatically, "You love her."

"That's beside the point."

"You didn't deny it," she pointed out. "You love her, Sammy?"

"What does love have to do with any of this, Ma?"

"It has everything to do with it. If you love her, you can't walk away from her or give up. You have to make her understand that you fear for her safety. You have to rescue her."

"How do you propose I do that when she's a hardheaded woman who won't listen to me?" he asked. "You can't rescue people who don't want to be rescued."

"If you love her, you'll find a way," she said. "You've allowed your fears to rob you of your candidacy. Don't let fear rob you of love, too, son."

He wanted to lie and tell his mother that he didn't love Alyson. But he couldn't. He did love her, though he hadn't admitted it to her.

"What difference does it make now? I'm here, she's there."

"And there are flights between here and there every day of the week."

"I came home to spend Christmas with you and the rest of the family."

"And your father?" she asked.

"He doesn't care if I'm here."

"He loves you, despite what you think, Sammy. He just has his way about things. He's set in his ways."

"He still blames me for not being a cop," said Samson. "I can't change who I am."

"Give him a chance."

"To hurt me again? I don't think so."

"Carve out some time to spend with him."

Samson gave his mother a sideways glance. Toni knew that he was just as stubborn as his father, and neither of them would give in to the other. Samson's dad was prideful and rigid. But Samson's heart was bigger, and he could be persuaded.

"For me?" she asked with a wink. "Can you do it for me?"

"I'll try." He kissed her cheek. "For you."

Toni Steel knew exactly how to appeal to Samson's heart.

# Chapter 21

Alyson had suddenly found herself in a position of choosing between her career and the man she'd become quite fond of. Going to her parents' home was exactly what she needed at the moment. She needed to see her father. Needed his advice—he was the best advice-giver she knew. She had no clue about how to handle the situation she'd found herself in, and her father was great at making sense of things. He'd know what to do.

She found him in his favorite position—on the front porch of their family home in Governor's Harbour, the Eleutheran newspaper in his lap, his reading glasses on his face, eyes closed and light snores escaping from his lips.

"Daddy," Alyson said and took a seat next to him.

"Hey." He smiled when he saw her. "I almost fell asleep out here."

"Almost?"

"Good thing I didn't."

"Yep, good thing." Alyson laughed at her father's antics. Then she sighed, remembering her purpose for the visit.

"What's on your mind?"

"Man troubles."

"Already?"

"What do you mean, 'already?'"

"The fellow… Jackson's friend," he said matter-of-factly. "Are you two already having troubles?"

"Is anything on this island sacred?"

"Very little."

"How do you choose between a man and your career?"

"I think that question would be better answered by your mother. She sacrificed her career for me," he said. "So I guess I'm somewhat biased."

"This is different."

She explained to her father about the Madisons, William Blue and Samson.

He removed his reading glasses, sat straight up in his chair and, with a look of concern, said, "Maybe you should listen to what he has to say. It appears that this could be a potentially dangerous situation."

"He's overreacting. I get that he was a victim, but you can't go around accusing innocent people of wrongdoing."

"Just be cautious is all I'm saying."

"I will, Daddy. But this is an important deal. This could make or break my real estate business," Alyson explained.

"And he must be a pretty important fellow if you're going through the fuss of it all."

"I like him a little," Alyson lied.

Her father was intuitive. "You'll make other business connections, but will you find a man that makes you smile like I've seen you smile lately? You haven't been happy for a long time, but you seem carefree now. You should consider that."

"Working with the Madisons can transform my career."

"No doubt, making a name for yourself in the industry is important," said Paul John Talbot, "but at what cost? Love?"

"Nobody said anything about love." Alyson was in denial.

"Well, you've found something. And you owe it to yourself to find out if that *something* is worth the fight."

"So just forget about everything that I've worked hard for?"

"I'm certainly not saying that. Being an achiever is who you are," he said. "But don't discount your heart."

"I think I've lost him, Daddy," said Alyson. "He caught a flight back to Chicago this afternoon."

"It's only geography, baby," said Paul John. "There are flights between here and there every day of the week."

Alyson looked at her phone when it buzzed. She opened the text message: Can you meet me this afternoon for a site visit?—Dustin.

She typed, I'm in the Caribbean.

Can you be in Miami by tomorrow afternoon? Say 2 pm?

Of course. She typed.

I'll arrange for an early morning flight and we can charge it to your new expense account. I'll be in touch soon with the details.

Thank you was all she could think to type.

When she looked up, she noticed her father observing her closely.

"Chicago fellow?" he asked.

"No. Business," she said. "I'm headed back to Miami in the morning."

"Then you should get a good night's sleep. Why don't you stay here, and I'll drive you to the airport in the morning."

She stood and kissed his cheek. "Anything good to eat in the kitchen?"

"Your mother always has something prepared. Go check things out." He gave her a wink.

"Thanks, Daddy, for listening to me."

"That's what I'm here for."

She rushed into the kitchen and found her mother's Bahamian spread. After finishing off a huge plate of grouper fish and pigeon peas with rice, she curled up on the sofa in the den. Surfed through the channels on the television and finally settled on a local news station. Thoughts of Samson filled her head. She missed him more than she was willing to admit. She longed for his kiss and touch. She missed his smile. Life with him had been glorious, though short-lived. Life without him was unbearable, uncomfortable. She was listless.

She dialed his number, and dared herself to press the send key. She couldn't. She wouldn't know what to say if he answered. And if he dismissed her, she'd be embarrassed. She was prideful.

She tossed the phone aside. Samson Steel would not get the opportunity to snub her twice in one lifetime. She would will herself not to think about him. Focus on business and forget he even existed. It was better that way.

# *Chapter 22*

Cecil Steel was the last person Samson wanted to see, but he'd promised his mother. His father was set in his ways. A man of average height, brown skin and graying hair, he was an older version of Samson. His father had been a thorn in his side since adolescence, since the first time Samson played an organized sport. He knew early on that he wouldn't be much of an athlete. He had no desire to play football or basketball. While his brothers excelled in both, Samson found greater pleasure in gaining knowledge. Learning became his sport.

"I thought I'd bring you out tonight, have a drink... spend some quality time with you, Pop."

"We could've had quality time at the house," said Cecil as he relaxed in the booth. "You don't need to take me to fancy restaurants to spend quality time with me, son. If you would just come by the house more often..."

"I didn't bring you here to argue."

His father placed reading glasses on his face and

grabbed the menu. Gave it a glance. "Have you seen these prices?"

"I eat here all the time, Pop. It's one of my favorite places," said Samson.

"A waste of good money," he mumbled, and continued to sift through the items on the menu.

"I recommend the shrimp and grits," Samson said. "Delicious!"

"Who eats shrimp with grits, and in the middle of the afternoon?" his father asked, peering at Samson over the top of his reading glasses.

"It's not all that unusual, Pop. I know lots of people who enjoy grits in the middle of the afternoon, as well as folks who eat fish for breakfast."

His thoughts drifted to the Bahamas and Alyson. She'd taught him to eat many things he hadn't experienced before. As much as he hated to admit it, he missed her. Couldn't get her out of his head.

"I've never heard of anyone eating fish for breakfast," said Cecil.

"It's because you live in a box, and you never step outside of it."

"It's not necessary to do all of these things that aren't going to make a bit of difference when you die," he said. "You love your family, and do the best you can in your career, and that's it."

"You love your family, huh? Does that mean all of your family, or just some?"

"Are you implying that I don't love you, Sammy?"

"I'm saying you don't respect me and my choices."

"Because your choices are absurd." He shut his menu and removed the glasses from his face. "For instance, you just got back from the Bahamas. The time you spent over there could've been time spent looking for another job. Did you forget that you're unemployed?"

"I needed a vacation," said Samson. "And besides, it's not like I'm broke. I can afford to take some time off. I need that."

"What you need is a career you can be proud of."

"I am proud of my career. At least the one I had," said Samson. "And I'm proud of my life, despite what you think."

"You don't seem proud at all. You seem confused," Cecil said.

"I'm not confused. I was a little distraught over what took place on the campaign trail, but I'm clear about what I want now."

"And what is it that you want?"

"I want to run again. In fact, I'm putting my campaign together for the next election."

"I never understood why you just didn't go into law enforcement, a meaningful career, like the rest of us."

"It's the same reason I didn't play football or basketball in high school, Pop. I have to do what makes me happy."

The server walked up, pad in hand, interrupting whatever Cecil was about to say.

"Are you gentlemen ready to order?" she asked.

Samson hadn't even taken a look at the menu. He didn't need to. Big Jones had always been one of his favorite restaurants, with its southern New Orleans cooking. He knew the menu like the back of his hand.

"I'll start with the crab cakes and a bowl of gumbo," Samson said. "And for my entrée I'll have the Carolina shrimp burger."

His father peered at him. "Hungry?"

"Famished," said Samson. He turned to the server. "Whatever the old man is having, put it on my tab."

"No. No. Young lady, I'll have my own tab, thank you," Cecil insisted.

Samson found pleasure in getting his father worked up. "And bring him a big fat order of the *boudin rouge*."

Samson laughed. He knew that his father would never order something that sounded so wicked. Although it was only Cajun sausage, Cecil Steel never veered outside his comfort zone. He'd either order the fried chicken or the fried catfish. Nothing that he couldn't pronounce.

"I don't even know what the hell that is, but I'm going to pass. I'll just have the fried chicken."

"Yes, sir." She smiled and grabbed both menus.

Samson snickered.

"Oh, you find that amusing, do you?" Cecil asked. "I don't know why we couldn't just go on over to the soul food place in our neighborhood. Why we have to go to this overpriced fancy-ass spot is beyond me."

"Because I want you to understand who I am."

"I know who you are! I raised you." His father took a sip of his iced water. "I gave your ass life."

"My mother gave me life," Samson said. "And you didn't quite raise me. You were never there. You were working all the time."

"A cop's job is never done. And I had to work to take care of my family," said Cecil. "You're not going to blame me for that, are you?"

"I blame you for not loving me unconditionally."

Cecil was unsettled in his seat. He adjusted his posture. "I love you in spite of your bad decisions. I'm hopeful that you'll figure things out one day. Before it's too late. You're getting too old for these shenanigans, Sammy."

Samson ignored his father's last comments. Getting through to him was a lost cause. And he knew that dinner had been a bad decision. His father would never respect anything he attempted in life, simply because he wasn't a cop. He could become the president of the United States, and Cecil Steel would find fault with it. It was just his way, and Samson had already made peace with that. His goal was to get through dinner with his father, and return to his loft. He wanted to be alone while brooding over missing Alyson.

## Chapter 23

Alyson met Dustin at an unfinished condominium development in Coral Gables. It was one that she was quite familiar with. She'd done market research in the area and already had a potential buyer in mind.

"There's quite a bit of buzz about this property," she told him.

"It's beautiful, with lots of amenities," he agreed. "Of course there's buzz!"

"Perfectly located," she said. "But the price is a little on the high side for the area."

"Madison properties are highly desirable, and they're priced accordingly."

"They are indeed, but we want to make sure our pricing is competitive, don't we?"

"If you check the comparables, we're not that far off," he said, and then changed the subject. "Sorry to pull you from your visit in the Caribbean, but Jonathan insisted that I show you around, bring you up to speed on our inventory."

"So you're more than just the finance guy," she said thoughtfully. "You show the properties, too?"

"I wear many hats," he said as he moved closer to her, and his hand slid to the small of her back. "Today, I'm your tour guide."

"As soon as I come on board, you won't have to show clients the inventory. I'll do that." She eased away from his touch. "Maybe we should move on to the next property."

She spent an uncomfortable remainder of the afternoon perusing Madison properties with Dustin. Some she'd already visited on her own, and most she'd researched online. A private tour wasn't necessary, in her opinion, but she obliged anyway. Particularly since Jonathan felt it was necessary. As the sun began to set, she could think of nothing more than retiring to her condo. She would order Chinese takeout and open a bottle of Riesling, try to drown the pain of missing Samson.

"Can I buy you dinner?" asked Dustin as he drove her to pick up her car at the office.

"Actually, I'm not hungry and I have plans. But thank you," she said.

"You have plans? With a boyfriend?" he asked.

"I think that's an inappropriate question, and I'm going to pretend that you didn't ask it," she said.

"I'm sorry," he said. "I'm just trying to figure you out. See if you're a good fit for the team."

She was grateful when he pulled into the parking lot next to her car.

She opened the passenger's door. "You have a good evening, Mr. Rose."

"I intend to," he said.

The moment she stepped into her car, she dialed Jonathan Madison.

"Hello, Mr. Madison. I'm sorry to bother you."

"No bother, Alyson. It's good to hear from you. I was going to ask you to drop by my office sometime this week so we can take a look at some properties. When will you be returning to Miami from the Caribbean?"

"I'm here now," she said. "I just met with Dustin at your request."

"At my request?"

"Yes. He flew me back here this afternoon. He said that you asked him to take me to a few sites," she said.

"That's strange. I haven't spoken with Dustin since the three of us had lunch together. But I'll give him a call and see what's going on. I'd like to have a sit-down with you and go over our inventory, whenever you have a moment."

"I can stop by in the morning."

"That sounds great. I'll meet you at my office at eight."

Her heart pounded rapidly. Her head began to spin. Dustin had lured her to Miami and had used Jonathan as an excuse. The thought of it gave her the creeps.

She tried to rid her thoughts of him as she entered her condo, flipped on the lights and removed her pumps. She collapsed onto the leather sofa and rested her head against the back of it. She couldn't quite put her finger on the source of the uneasiness she felt in her gut. She didn't know if it was her new relationship with Madison Development that was causing her the most angst, or Dustin Rose himself.

She pulled her cell phone from her purse, dialed the number for her favorite Asian spot and ordered dinner. She opened a bottle of Riesling and poured herself a glass. After changing into a pair of sweats and a T-shirt, she pulled her laptop out of its bag and spread paperwork all over the sofa, then got lost in her work.

Phones were constantly ringing, and conversations permeated the office of Madison Development Company.

She'd dressed carefully in one of her most conservative pantsuits. If she bumped into Dustin, she didn't want him to misunderstand their interaction again. Not like the last time they'd met. He'd thought it fitting to say inappropriate things to her in their last meeting, and to touch the small of her back without her permission.

"I'm here to see Jonathan Madison," she told the receptionist.

"He was expecting you, Miss Talbot, but he got called to one of our sites. He asked me to apologize profusely and to reschedule with you."

"It's okay, Carol. I'll take over for Jonathan," said Dustin, who appeared out of nowhere. "You can step into my office, Miss Talbot."

She reluctantly followed Dustin down the hallway and into his office. He motioned for her to have a seat. She slid into the leather seat across from his desk.

"I think Jonathan just wanted to bring you up to speed on the inventory. He wanted us to go ahead and sign a listing agreement—document your relationship with us as our agent." He pulled a contract from his file cabinet.

"I spoke with Jonathan yesterday about our little housing tour. He didn't ask you to fly me back here and take me on a tour yesterday. In fact, he didn't even know anything about it."

"Of course he did." Dustin laughed nervously.

"No, he didn't. He thought I was still in the Bahamas."

"The old man is starting to forget things," said Dustin. "Which is why I've suggested that he seriously think about retiring. He's been doing this for a long time, and he's starting to slip. I think he should go enjoy his family and his wealth and leave the hard work to us young folk."

"So you're telling me that he asked you to fly me back here to Miami to visit properties, and then he forgot about it?"

"That's exactly what I'm telling you," Dustin said. "Jonathan is a great man, but he's forgetful. Just like he forgot that he had another commitment before scheduling a meeting with you this morning."

She had thought that odd. Had something really come up, or had Jonathan Madison forgotten about their conversation?

"I don't know what games you're playing, Mr. Rose, but I'm not the one to play with," she warned.

"I don't have time for games, Alyson," he said. "Can I call you Alyson?"

"Call me Miss Talbot."

"I'm a busy man, Miss Talbot. And this is a busy office. Jonathan Madison doesn't have time to worry about the little details of running this company. Which is why I'm here. I free him to handle other things."

"You can just give me the listing contract. I'll take a look at it and bring it back over later." Alyson stood.

"It's just your standard listing agreement, Miss Talbot."

"As I said, I'll take a look and bring it back when I meet with Jonathan."

"That's fine," said Dustin. "No worries."

"And by the way, I have a potential buyer for the Coral Gables property. I'd like to see if we could get him prequalified through your preferred lender as soon as possible."

"We'll take a look at it, just as soon as we get a signed copy of that listing agreement." He came around and sat on the edge of his desk right in front of her.

"Fine." She walked toward the door.

"Welcome to the team, Alyson." He failed to use her professional name.

She left without another word.

She slipped into her car and relaxed into the seat. Alyson was a strong person. She didn't back down to anyone, and she didn't allow people to get under her skin. But Dustin Rose was under her skin. She didn't like him, and she was uneasy about working with him. She thought that she'd be happy about Madison Development, but so far she'd been everything but. She carefully backed the car out of the parking space and simultaneously answered her ringing phone with the push of a button.

"Jules, what's up?"

"I did some research on that Dustin Rose fellow like you asked," she said. "He has quite the history."

"Does he now?"

"He's connected to a laundry list of scandals, from unethical real estate deals to bribery."

"Are you kidding?"

"Not in the least," said Jules. "It pays to have private detectives as friends. Especially friends who owe you favors. This guy Dustin is a piece of work, to say the least. He went before a judge in Illinois and somehow managed to get probation for the bribery charge. Left the company that he worked for in Chicago and moved here. Turns out, he knew some people. He was able to land a job at Madison Development without so much as a background check. He's been here for less than a year now."

"What was the name of the company he worked for in Chicago?" She already knew the answer, but needed to hear it anyway.

"Let me see," Jules said as she riffled through some pages. "Blue Island Properties."

An unsettling feeling rested in the pit of Alyson's stomach. At that moment, she knew that Samson's suspicions were correct.

"That's not all," said Jules.

"There's more?" She was afraid to hear the rest.

"They're using straw buyers to get these deals pushed

through the lender," she said. "You're not under a listing agreement with them, are you?"

"I haven't signed one yet."

"Don't sign anything with them. My advice is to cut all ties."

"Samson was right."

"Who's Samson?" Jules asked. "The mystery man you haven't told me anything about?"

"Yes. He probably hates me now. I've messed up everything," said Alyson. "And now he's gone back to Chicago, and I'll probably never see him again."

"Do you need me to find him, too?"

"No. I just need to put on my big girl panties and call him."

"Go get your man, girl!" Jules said.

Alyson was beginning to rethink everything she thought Madison Development was or wasn't. She'd come from a good Bahamian family with strong values, and she knew that a company built on unethical behavior would never last. Good companies were built on strong foundations, and Alyson Talbot and Associates wouldn't be the exception. As much as she needed the hefty commissions and the exposure, she knew what she had to do. Besides that, she needed her man. However, she'd already dismissed him. To win him back meant admitting that she was wrong, which was something that wasn't easy for her. But she was willing to do it. She wasn't sure if he'd welcome her with open arms, but she needed to try. She needed to make amends with the man she loved.

Yes, *loved.*

Before it was too late.

# *Chapter 24*

Nat King Cole crooned about chestnuts roasting on an open fire. The house smelled of gingerbread. Garland and scented candles rested upon the mantel. Samson opened the door as wide as he could get it and held on to the trunk of the tree, while his father pushed the branches inside from the other end.

"Oh, my, what a beautiful tree! Y'all picked a good one," his mother raved. She pointed toward the corner of the room, near the fireplace, where Christmas trees had always been set up for most of Samson's life. "Set it up right over here, baby. You know the spot."

Samson steadied the tree on its stand, while his father tightened the screws. The smell of pine filled his nose. Needles from the tree bounced against the polished hardwoods. He let go of the tree and then stood back, marveling at how beautiful it was. He and his father *had* picked a good one. It was the one thing they'd agreed on that day, that the eastern white pine was the perfect tree.

"Cecil, come with me to the basement to grab the skirt and decorations," Toni said.

Cecil groaned but followed his wife.

"I'll come, too, Grandmother!" Samson's ten-year-old niece, Natalie, followed her grandparents.

"Good to see you, Sammy." Samson's older brother, Jessie, reached for a handshake. "I was wondering if you'd be home for Christmas."

"Are you growing a beard, or you just too lazy to shave?" Samson asked Jessie.

Jessie grinned widely and rubbed the hair on his face. "You like it?"

"Makes you look old."

"Makes me look distinguished," Jessie said. "What about your beard?"

"Mine isn't nearly as rustic."

"My wife likes it. Right, babe?" Jessie asked Patricia as she entered the room from the kitchen.

"The beard has got to go! Please talk to your brother, Samson. Please tell him to cut it. Yours is perfect. But this right here, a hot mess," said Patricia. She gave Samson a strong embrace. "Good to see you."

Samson's younger brother burst through the front door, his daughter in tow. Calvin stomped the snow from his boots on the rug, and Olivia followed suit. She removed her wool hat and rushed toward Samson.

"Uncle Sammy!" the six-year-old exclaimed before jumping into his arms.

He held his niece tightly in his arms and kissed her plump cheek. "Who's your favorite uncle in the world?" he asked.

"You are!" she shouted.

"What?" Jessie asked Olivia. "Then what am I?"

"You're my favorite, too, Uncle Jessie," said Olivia, who rested her head on Samson's shoulder.

"Well, if it isn't Sammy Steel!" Calvin embraced his brother. "Nice tree, chump. Glad she didn't ask me to go with the old man to pick it out. I bet it was a horrible experience."

"I went last year," said Jessie. "It was a painful process. He's anal."

"Actually, it wasn't all that bad," said Samson. "But you're right, he's anal about everything. I took him to dinner, and all he did was complain."

"Here we go!" Toni placed a box filled with decorations in the center of the floor. "Let's get to decorating. You know this is my favorite Christmas tradition, decorating the tree with you guys."

Cecil plopped down in his easy chair in the corner of the room. He never helped decorate, only watched. He'd done his due diligence by picking out the tree and bringing it home. It was his philosophy for everything. *I'll bring it home—you deal with it from there.*

Toni began to decorate with bulbs, lights and garland. The children placed their handmade ornaments onto the branches. Samson and his brothers drank beers and tried talking louder than the music, until it was time to place the star at the top of the tree. It was a tradition for the youngest member of the Steel clan to do the honors of situating the star in its rightful place.

"Higher, Uncle Sammy!" Olivia squealed . Her legs dangled against Samson's chest as he lifted her in the air. "Lift me higher."

"Yeah, higher, Uncle Sammy!" Calvin teased.

"You should be over here lifting your own daughter," Samson said to Calvin. "Why do I have to be the designated person to lift these little rug rats on my shoulders every year?"

"I'm not a rug rat, Uncle Sammy!"

"No, you're not. And I'm sorry for calling you that." Samson kissed his niece's ashy knee apologetically.

"You're the designated child-lifter because you're tall," Calvin said. "You're the tall one, and I'm the smart, handsome one. Everybody knows that."

"The smart, handsome one." Samson laughed.

"And when you're done with your Christmas tree duties, I'm sure Ma has some other duties she'd like for you to perform," Calvin said.

"That's fine. And while I'm performing my Christmas tree duties, you can run on down to Albertson's Supermarket and pick up the canned milk and sweet potatoes so that Ma can make her famous sweet potato pie," Samson said.

"I believe she asked you to go to the store," Calvin asserted. "If I remember correctly, sweet potato pie is your favorite, not mine."

"I would go, but I'm busy right now." Samson shrugged. "Christmas tree duties."

"We could live without sweet potato pie," Toni interjected. "We have plenty of other sweets in there—pecan pie, a chocolate cake, banana pudding…"

"Besides, the streets are getting pretty slick out there," added their father.

"The streets aren't that bad yet, Pop," said Samson. "And, Ma, what is Christmas tree decorating without sweet potato pie?"

"It is his favorite," said Toni.

"My car is blocked in the driveway anyway. I would need to shovel my way out, and I'm hardly in the mood for shoveling," Calvin countered, and then plopped down on the sofa next to their mother, gave her a light kiss on the cheek. He was more of a mama's boy than Samson was.

Samson dug into the pocket of his jeans and retrieved his keys, then tossed them to Calvin. With a wicked grin on his face he said, "Take mine, I'm parked on the street."

"Not this time, big bro." Calvin tossed the keys back.

Samson gave in. He put on his wool coat, bundling it as tightly as he could. He placed a toboggan hat on his head and secured a woven scarf around his neck. "Ma, is there anything else you need besides canned milk and sweet potatoes?"

"A chocolate bar!" exclaimed Olivia.

"Okay, canned milk, sweet potatoes and a chocolate bar," Samson said as he headed for the door. "Even though chocolate bars will rot your teeth, I'll bring you one."

Samson loved his niece and thought that she was Calvin's greatest achievement. He'd been a screwup most of his life, but Olivia had changed all of that. She was the one thing that kept Calvin focused. He'd become a master at single parenting after the child's mother had abandoned her.

Samson's boots slid against the concrete on the front porch. Whatever was falling had already turned to ice. He made it to the two-door sedan, got inside and slammed the door. He drove slowly down their parents' block, the same block that he'd grown up on, played kickball in the middle of the street and tossed a football to his brothers more times than he could remember.

His phone buzzed, and he struggled to pull it from the pocket of his jeans. He looked at the screen and was surprised to see Alyson's number. He'd wanted to call her a million times, but hadn't built up the nerve. They hadn't ended on a good note, and he didn't know how to make things right between them. He missed the call, but vowed that he'd call her back at a better time.

In the middle of the block he picked up speed, misjudging the roads. When he made it to the end of the street, he lost control and drove right through the stop sign, not even hesitating. Samson was in a state of shock as he dropped the phone and slammed head-on into a truck moving in the opposite direction.

# Chapter 25

The yellow cab eased down Congress Parkway, and then pulled up in front of the historical brick building. Alyson reached into her purse for cash, but then realized she only had Bahamian bills.

"Shit," she whispered under her breath. "You take credit cards?"

"Yes, ma'am," the Ethiopian driver said.

She hated using her plastic in cities that were unfamiliar, and for a cab ride no less. But she didn't have a choice in the matter. She paid the driver and then stepped out of the car, wearing her Pedro Garcia boots with the peep toe. She'd underestimated the weather in Chicago and wished she'd worn a much heavier coat. The designer leather trench coat was neither practical nor warm. She shivered as the driver placed her Gucci luggage on wheels at the curb.

She stepped inside the brick building and pulled her

notes from her purse to double-check the unit number. She was surprised to learn that the elevator was broken in such a nice building, and that she'd be taking the stairs in her leather boots. She stood in front of the unit with her fist raised. She was about to knock, when the door swung opened and a man with a strong resemblance to Samson appeared in the doorway.

"May I help you?" he asked.

"I'm looking for Samson Steel," she said.

"He's not here at the moment," said the tall, handsome man. "Who can I say is looking for him?"

"I'm Alyson Talbot. A dear friend of his—"

"Alyson." He smiled. "You're much prettier than he described."

"And you are?"

"I'm Calvin. His brother." He opened the door wider. "Why don't you step inside?"

"When do you expect him to return?" She glanced around at the meticulous space. It was quintessential Samson.

"The doctors are saying a few days, but you know Sammy's impatient ass! He's ready to come home now."

"Excuse me." She had no idea what Calvin was rambling on about. "What is this about doctors?"

"He's in the hospital," Calvin said matter-of-factly. "Still recovering from the accident."

"Oh, my God! What accident?"

"You didn't know?" he asked. "There was some trauma to his head, and a broken collarbone…"

"Where can I find him?"

"He's at Mercy Hospital," said Calvin. "I dropped by his place to pick him up some fresh clothes. I can give you a ride over there if you give me a minute."

"That would be great. Thank you."

* * *

She was disconcerted when she saw him. A bandage was on his shoulder, and his eyes were lightly closed. She stood in the corner for a moment and observed him sleeping. Her heart ached for him.

It was her fault that he was there. Had he remained in the Bahamas, the accident would never have taken place. She felt tears welling up. He opened his eyes.

"Hey, love," he said softly and smiled. "What are you doing here?"

"I'm so sorry."

"For what?"

"You were right all along. About Madison."

"I didn't want to be right."

"I'm sorry I didn't listen to you. I was being stubborn, only thinking of myself."

"I was only thinking of you, sweetheart, and your well-being. I hoped for the best, but had a bad feeling in my gut."

"I wish I'd listened. Maybe you wouldn't have left the islands, and you wouldn't be in this predicament." The tears crept down her face. "You're here because of me."

"I'm here because I underestimated the ice storm." He held his hand out. "Come here."

She walked over to him. She leaned in and kissed his lips. "I've missed you."

"Not as much as I've missed you." He held her tightly in his arms.

She felt safe there, didn't want to let him go. She composed herself, and then walked over to the window and opened the blinds to let some daylight into the room.

When Samson observed her clothing and boots, he chuckled. "You wore that here?"

"Don't judge me. I've never been to Chicago." She laughed, too.

"Obviously. You look gorgeous, and those boots are nice, but not very practical." He laughed, and it hurt. "We'll have to go to Walmart when I get out of here and get you some warmer clothing."

"Fine." She smiled through her tears, then went back to his arms. "I can't wait for you to get out of here."

His parents walked into the room, and stopped in their tracks when they saw the embrace.

"Well, hello," said Toni. "I didn't know you had company, Sammy."

Alyson stood. Straightened her clothing.

"Ma, this is Alyson. Alyson, my parents—Toni and Cecil Steel."

"So nice to meet you, sweetheart." She shook Alyson's hand, and then behind her back gave Samson an exaggerated wink.

"Pleased to you meet you, Alyson. We've heard absolutely nothing about you," said Cecil.

"I heard about her," Toni countered.

"So great to meet you both."

"You live here in Chicago?" Cecil asked.

"No, sir, I live in Miami."

"You came all the way here from Miami?" he asked, a puzzled expression on his face.

"She's from the Bahamas, Cecil," Toni boasted. "This is the young lady Sammy met while he was over there."

"Oh, when he was over there wasting time doing nothing," said Cecil.

"Don't start, Cecil," Toni warned.

"So you're from the Bahamas, but you live in Miami." Cecil was attempting to piece the details together.

"Hello." Samson interrupted the interaction between

his parents. They were talking about him as if he wasn't in the room. "So glad to see you both."

"I brought you some fried catfish, baby." Toni handed Samson a brown paper bag. "I know the food here can't be that great."

Cecil took a seat in the corner of the room. "I thought Calvin was bringing you clean clothes," he said.

"He went downstairs to the cafeteria for a cup of coffee," Alyson offered.

"You met Calvin?" Samson asked her.

"He brought me over here. I went to your loft first. Had no idea that you were in the hospital. Calvin was there."

"Whatever he said about me, don't believe a word of it," Samson said.

Calvin walked in on the tail end of the conversation. "I only speak the truth."

"He's been jealous of me his whole life," Samson teased.

"Is that Mama's catfish I'm smelling?" He reached for the brown paper bag.

"Get your paws back, bro," said Samson. "Reach for my catfish and draw back a nub."

"He's always been so selfish," Calvin told Alyson. "I don't know what you see in him."

Alyson giggled. She loved the banter between Samson and his brother.

"How long will you be staying, honey?" Toni asked Alyson.

"I don't know. Until he's better." She smiled at Samson.

"You're welcome to stay at the house with us. I'll fix up Sammy's old room for you," said Toni.

"She can stay at my loft, Ma. She'd probably be more comfortable there."

"I'm going to stay right here with Samson until he leaves. I don't want to leave his side."

"That's so sweet." Toni grabbed Alyson's hand.

"I love that accent," said Calvin. "You have any sisters or cousins who talk like that?"

"She's an only child," Samson lied with a grin.

"She's not an only child," said Calvin. "You just told me that her sister was getting married on Christmas Day."

"Damn! I did, didn't I?" said Samson.

"Oh, how romantic. A Christmas wedding in the Bahamas," said Toni. "If your sister looks anything like you, she's going to be a beautiful bride."

"Thank you." Alyson smiled at Toni.

"Well, let's get going, Cecil," Toni said. "Give these lovebirds some privacy. I'm sure they've got some catching up to do. And I need to finish my Christmas shopping."

Cecil stood and grabbed Calvin's foam cup filled with coffee.

"Pop, that's my coffee."

"Mine now," said Cecil as he headed for the door. "Pleasure to meet you, Alyson."

"Likewise, sir," said Alyson.

"Lovely meeting you, sweetheart." Toni gave Alyson a warm smile. "Make sure you bring her by the house, Sammy. And take her to Walmart and buy her some warm clothing."

"'Bye, Ma," said Samson.

Toni grabbed the sleeve of Calvin's coat. "Let's go, Calvin."

"I'm coming."

"Love you, baby," Toni said to Samson as she walked out of the room.

"Love you, too, Ma."

Alyson crawled up into the bed with Samson. She told him everything that had occurred in her world since he was gone. And how she wished she'd taken heed of his warning. She needed him to fix what had been broken. His heart ached because he hadn't been there when she needed him the most, to protect her—to make things right.

"When you didn't answer my call the other day and didn't return it, I thought I'd lost you," she explained.

"It was the day I had the accident. I saw the call just before I slid into an 18-wheeler."

She pressed her hand against his face. "I was miserable without you. Can you forgive me for being so hard-headed?"

"Forgiven."

He kissed her lips. He'd come back home with intentions of staying and organizing his campaign. He didn't know where he would go from here, but he knew that wherever it was, he wanted Alyson Talbot right by his side.

## Chapter 26

Alyson streamed Christmas lights around the leaves of the ficus tree. Samson rested his back against the leather sofa, an afghan thrown across his legs. The loft smelled of Bahamian spices. Alyson was overjoyed that she finally had an opportunity to cook for her man and his family. She stirred the cabbage and pulled the Bahamian macaroni and cheese from the oven. The fried chicken was perfectly golden brown, and the grouper fish was seasoned to perfection while it baked in the oven.

She sipped on a glass of sky juice and handed Samson one.

"I don't think my home has ever smelled this good," said Samson.

"Dinner's almost done," she said. "And your family will be here shortly."

"We can call them and cancel if you want. They're a dysfunctional bunch of folks, and I would understand if you changed your mind."

"After I cooked all of this food? Don't be silly!" She laughed. "They can't be any more dysfunctional than my family."

"Believe me, they are," he told her. "My brothers certainly have their issues. Calvin's divorced and raising his daughter alone. Jessie is married but threatening to leave every other week. Why get married if you're planning to walk away every time you turn around?"

"I agree."

"That's not happening to me. When I get married, it's forever."

"Me, too."

It was as if they were talking about each other, but not directly. Testing the waters. Marriage had never been a subject that he and Alyson had discussed.

Samson changed the subject. "Besides everyone else, my father is the most ornery person on the face of the earth."

"I didn't get that vibe from him. He seemed so sweet."

"He was on his best behavior in front of you," said Samson. "He has a low opinion of me, and makes it a point to let me know it every chance he gets. He wanted me to be a cop and, because I didn't, he thinks that I'm worthless."

"He doesn't think you're worthless."

"He does," Samson insisted. "All my life, I've had to work for his approval. And I've never gotten it. Finally I stopped looking for it."

"I'm sorry, baby."

"It's cool. I don't try so hard now," said Samson. "My mother tries to place us in these situations where we have to bond or spend quality time. I try to make her happy, but I've come to terms with the inevitable. He's never going to be proud of anything I do."

"He's proud," she said. "Maybe he just has a hard time expressing it."

"Maybe," Samson said. "I don't care anymore. Remind me to never treat my son that way."

"So you're planning to have a son someday?"

"If you're asking me if I want children, of course I do," he said. "At least a dozen."

"A dozen kids?"

"Okay, maybe five," he said. "All boys."

"Five?"

"Okay, maybe not quite that many. But all boys for sure," he reiterated.

"No girls?"

"Girls are too high maintenance for my taste. Too emotional and too much baggage." He smirked. "Look how much trouble you are."

"I'm not that bad."

"Your father's hair is completely gray. And I'm willing to bet it's because of you and your sisters."

"I beg your pardon." Alyson tossed a pillow at Samson. "I didn't give my parents any trouble at all. I did everything by the book."

"A Goody Two-shoes," he said matter-of-factly.

"Pretty much."

Samson pulled her down onto the sofa, held her tightly. She stretched her body on top of him. Her lips kissed his, and his tongue danced inside of hers. His fingertips began to gently caress her breasts. He started to unbutton her blouse, and she grabbed his hand.

"Your family will be here in a minute," she whispered as the doorbell chimed.

"Damn," he said. "We'll pick up where we left off later."

Alyson adjusted her clothing before heading to the door. She opened it.

Toni kissed her on the cheek and handed her a pie. "I brought sweet potato pie for Sammy, seeing as how I didn't get to make him one," she said. "Oh, my, it smells so good in here!"

"Hello, Alyson." Cecil reached for her hand. "Good seeing you again."

"You, too, Mr. Steel." She bypassed his handshake and gave him a hug.

Just as she was about to shut the door, Calvin pushed it open. "I brought Cognac!" He held a bottle of Hennessy into the air and kissed Alyson's cheek.

Olivia rushed past her father and jumped onto the sofa with Samson. "Uncle Sammy!"

"Careful, now. Your uncle Sammy's shoulder is hurt," Toni told her granddaughter.

Alyson reached for Calvin's bottle to take it to the kitchen, but he tightened his grip.

"I'll hold on to it for now." He smiled.

Samson kissed his niece's forehead. "Alyson, this pretty lady is Olivia."

Alyson reached for the little girl's hand. "Pleased to meet you, Olivia."

"Are you going to marry my uncle Sammy?" Olivia asked.

All eyes were on Alyson. Everyone seemed to want an answer to that very question.

"Well, I don't know." Alyson glanced at Samson, who gave her an inquisitive look. "You'll have to ask him."

"Maybe one day," said Samson.

The doorbell interrupted an uneasy moment, and Alyson started toward the door.

"I'll get it," said Calvin. "It's just Jessie and his family. I saw them pull up after I did, but they were arguing so I didn't stick around."

Jessie walked in with his daughter, Natalie, and greeted everyone. His wife, Patricia, came in a few seconds afterward. Her eyes were red.

"Is this guy still faking an injury?" Jessie asked, motioning toward Samson. "And you must be Alyson."

"Yes, hello." Alyson shook Jessie's hand.

"I'm Jessie, Samson's older, better-looking brother," he said. "And this is my daughter, Natalie."

"Pleased to meet you both."

Patricia rolled her eyes at her husband for not introducing her. "I'm Patricia, Alyson. So glad to meet you."

"And you." Alyson shook the woman's hand and gave her a gentle smile.

"We need music," Calvin announced, and reached for the remote to Samson's stereo. He muted the television.

"You don't even care that the Chicago Bears are playing right now?" asked Cecil.

"Pop, they're down by thirty points, and it's the fourth quarter." Calvin started his hip-hop playlist despite his father's protests.

"I'm going to check on dinner," Alyson said, heading for the kitchen.

"I'll give you a hand, sweetheart." Toni followed. "You've got it smelling so good in here."

"Thank you," said Alyson as she pulled the fish from the oven.

"Everything looks so good!" Toni exclaimed. "Where'd you learn to cook?"

"My mother. She made sure we all learned how to cook when we were growing up."

"So many young girls these days don't have a clue about cooking, cleaning or raising children."

Patricia walked into the kitchen. "Can I help you do anything, Alyson?"

"If we could just get the table set," Alyson said. "Samson only has table settings for four, so we'll have to use paper products."

"He's been a bachelor for so long," Toni said. "He needs a woman who knows her way around a kitchen."

"I haven't seen Sammy smile so much," Patricia added. "I used to make Jessie smile like that, but lately things haven't been so good."

"Marriage is tough, baby." Toni rested her hand against Patricia's face. "And Jessie isn't the easiest person to get along with."

"I try so hard, Mom."

"I know, baby," said Toni. She grabbed the stack of plates from Alyson and went to set the dining room table.

"Samson is a sweetheart," Patricia whispered to Alyson. "I've been around a long time. Jessie and I were high school sweethearts. And I've seen women come and go in Sammy's life, but none have ever made him smile like he has since meeting you."

Alyson's heart danced, but she kept a straight face. She and Patricia carried dishes filled with food to the table. Cecil had managed to steal the stereo's remote control from Calvin, and the music had changed from hip-hop to old school. Marvin Gaye's "What's Going On" began to amplify through the speakers.

"Come on, Cecil, dance with me," said Toni.

"I don't feel like dancing, Antionette," Cecil protested.

"Oh, come on! Let's show these young people how it's done," she insisted, and pulled her husband up from the chair.

Cecil rolled his eyes, but joined his wife in the middle of the floor. Alyson watched with admiration as the two of them slow danced. They reminded her of her own parents, and she smiled. She glanced over at Samson, who was also watching his parents with the same admiration. She caught his eye, and he gave her a smile and a wink.

Her heart was so full of joy at that moment. There was nothing more satisfying than good music, a good meal, family, and the man that she was quickly falling head over heels in love with.

# Chapter 27

Toni washed pots, pans and glasses by hand. Soapy suds covered her arms, and a dish towel was draped over her shoulder.

"You know, we could've just loaded those dishes into this overpriced, state-of-the-art dishwasher," Alyson told Toni.

"I hate dishwashers. I always wash by hand," Toni said with a smile.

"I could've done this," said Alyson.

"You did enough, young lady. Dinner was fabulous. You're a great cook, and such a beautiful young woman," she said. "I've certainly enjoyed meeting you."

"And I've enjoyed meeting you."

"I don't know you very well, but I have good intuition about people. You're good and wholesome," said Toni. "What are your plans? Are you staying around here for a while?"

"I have to get back to the Bahamas soon. My sister's

wedding is fast approaching," Alyson explained. "And I've got some loose ends to tie up with my business in Miami."

"You're a busy woman. Where does that leave you and Sammy?"

Alyson shrugged. "I don't know. I guess we'll take things a day at a time."

Toni handed Alyson the last glass to dry. She dried her hands on the towel. "I hope to see you again real soon," she said.

Alyson followed Toni into the living room, where Samson and his father were enjoying the last few minutes of a football game together.

"Let's go, Cecil!"

"It's three minutes left on the clock," Cecil protested.

"We have to go. It's late, and these kids want some privacy." Toni grabbed Cecil's wool topcoat and handed it to him.

Cecil groaned, but stood. Toni secured the buttons on her coat and wrapped a knit scarf around her neck. She placed a matching knit hat onto her head. Samson stood and walked with his mother to the door.

"I like her," Toni whispered when she and Samson were alone.

"Love you, Ma." Samson kissed his mother's cheek. He was overjoyed by his mother's comment. He'd hoped that Alyson and his mother would get along.

"Dinner was wonderful, Alyson," said Cecil.

"Thank you," said Alyson as she gave Cecil a hug.

"Safe travels when you return home, sweetheart," Toni told Alyson.

"Thank you and good night," Alyson said.

She found her place next to Samson as he wrapped his arm around her shoulder.

"Tonight was good. The dysfunctional people approved of you," said Samson. "You know what that means, right?"

"No, what?"

"You're just as dysfunctional as they are."

"Your family is sweet. And very normal."

"There's nothing normal about them." Samson found his way to Alyson's lips and kissed them gently. He balanced himself against the wall and pulled her into him. "Let's finish what we started before they got here."

Alyson followed Samson into the bedroom. He gently lay on the king-size bed. Alyson carefully pulled his T-shirt over his head and began to plant soft kisses along his muscular chest. She loosened his sweatpants from around his waist and pulled them down. Samson assisted as much as he could until he was wearing only boxer shorts. She undid the buttons on her silk blouse and unbuttoned her jeans. She slid the jeans over her hips and let her blouse slide from her shoulders. She loosened the clasp on her front-hook red bra and freed her breasts.

Samson became aroused while watching her. He reached for her breasts and squeezed each one tenderly. He lifted himself up and placed one into his mouth, and she moaned as he nibbled on it. Alyson kissed his neck and chest and worked her way down to his navel. She reached for him, began to caress him through his boxer shorts. She removed his shorts, and her lips found his.

When Alyson felt Samson inside of her, she knew that life without him would be unacceptable.

She watched as the snow fell outside. As daylight crept through the window, she pulled the thick comforter close to her chin. She'd completely underestimated Chicago weather. Even with Samson's thick socks hugging her feet, and his light blue, tailored dress shirt buttoned all the way up to her neck, she was still cold. She wished she'd taken him up on that trip to Walmart for some insulated sleep pants, as she struggled to keep her legs warm.

Samson grabbed her from behind. "What are you thinking, love?"

"That I've never seen snow before."

"Never?"

"Well, on television and in movies. But never in real life."

"And what do you think about it?"

"I can live without being out there in it. I love looking at it from this window, though."

"You ready to go back to the Bahamas?"

She turned to face him. Placed her hand against his face. "I need to wrap things up with Jazzy's wedding. Christmas is in a few weeks."

"Will you come back?" he asked.

"To this weather? I can't live in Chicago, and my work is still in Miami. Even after I cut ties with Madison Development, I'm still in the process of building my business."

"Where does that leave us, then? Because I can't live without you in my life."

"It puts us in a difficult situation," she said.

"It certainly does."

"I'm sorry I didn't have your back before. I should've trusted you," she told him.

"Yes, you should've."

"I need you," she found herself saying. She couldn't believe she'd actually said those words to another human being.

"What about your career? What about Alyson Talbot and Associates?"

"You were right about the Madisons," she admitted.

"Besides it wouldn't make any sense to gain all the wealth in the world, but lose the man I love in the end."

"Did you say love?"

"Okay, yes. I love you," she admitted, "but let's not dwell on it."

"You've never said that to a man before, have you?"

"Only once. And it was a very long time ago."

He pulled her closer, and his lips met hers. His kiss sealed the deal, and the return was far better than any commission she'd made on any deal.

Her return flight home was long and emotional. She left Chicago not knowing where her relationship with Samson stood. She knew that she could never relocate, and his political career was calling him back to Illinois. He had already begun to arrange his campaign. Her home was in Florida, his was in Illinois and neither of them was willing to change that fact.

She leaned her head against the seat. Earbuds were plugged into her ears, and a magazine lay facedown in her lap. She tried reading, but kept becoming distracted. Thoughts of Samson rushed through her mind, and she wondered if she'd left too soon. She wanted to spend Christmas with the man she loved, but she had other priorities in the Bahamas. Jasmine was depending on her, and she wouldn't let her down.

# *Chapter 28*

The altar was decorated with Christmas orchids and beautiful red poinsettias. The baby grand piano was garnished with fragrant red and white candles. Little bouquets of fresh red roses and calla lilies were sprinkled with Christmas greens and hypericum berries and strategically placed around the room, while sweet Bahamian music played softly.

Alyson stood at the altar, as her heart was filled with joy. She watched as Jackson stood on the other side of the altar and awaited his bride. She gave him a comforting smile. He needed it because he was nervous. Sweat beaded on his forehead, and he fidgeted with his hands.

Jasmine was a beautiful bride, dressed in the gown that she'd chosen in Miami. It was perfect. As she glided down the aisle, Alyson couldn't help but feel a great deal of happiness for her sister—and pride. Jasmine had found love. Alyson dabbed the tears from her eyes with a handkerchief as she watched her father deliver her sister to her knight in shining armor. Before Samson waltzed into her life, she'd never even considered marriage for herself, but she had to admit, it wasn't completely out of the question. She could see herself in a similar perfect gown—not necessarily a Vera Wang one, but a perfect one. A gown that would speak to her like her mother said it would.

Suddenly she understood her mother's sacrifices. She knew that love changed things, and she wouldn't judge her mother ever again. Samson had transformed her mind and heart. She'd been married to her career for years, but now she could finally see herself married to a man. She would make the sacrifice, even if it meant uprooting her business and relocating to a new city.

Alyson glanced over at her mother, who was also dabbing tears from her eyes. Her father gave her mother a quick kiss on the cheek, and Alyson couldn't help but smile. Her parents had found love at a young age. And her mother had sacrificed her career for the man of her dreams. She quickly realized that love sometimes went hand in hand with sacrifice.

While Jackson and Jasmine exchanged vows, Alyson smiled with pride. Her heart was filled with joy for them. Jasmine handed her the bouquet of white roses to hold while she kissed her groom. Everyone applauded when Pastor Johnson introduced the new husband and wife to the congregation.

"I now present to you Mr. and Mrs. Jackson Conner."

The couple faced their guests and took their long stride back down the aisle—this time together.

Alyson watched the dance floor fill up as couples danced to the sound of the Caribbean band Onyx.

"Do you need me to dance with you?" asked Edward. He was dressed in a handsome tuxedo, the jacket draped over his shoulder.

"Of course not."

"Well, you're sitting here looking all sad and desolate."

"I'm fine."

"She's missing her boo," said Whitney.

"Who is her boo?" Alyson's younger brother, Nate, asked.

Alyson's brother Nate had flown in from Atlanta the night before. The family hadn't seen him since the Grove's grand opening, and probably wouldn't see him again for another year. Nate was determined never to return to the islands long-term, and he wouldn't stay for visits very long. The Bahamas held too many bad memories for him. Memories of being jilted by his high school sweetheart still haunted him. The Bahamas, his home, was a constant reminder of that. But he would never miss Jasmine's wedding. Jasmine and Nate had been comrades their entire lives.

"Her boo is Samson Steel, Jackson's handsome friend," Whitney explained.

"And why isn't he here?" Nate asked.

"He went back to Chicago," said Whitney.

"Can we please stop discussing my business as if I'm not standing here?"

"I'll go grab you a glass of wine," said Edward. "You want white or red?"

"White's fine," said Alyson.

"I'm going to check on Mother," said Whitney. "She was hoping that Denny would make it home for the wedding. It's sad he's not here."

"I was hoping Denny would make it home, too. Maybe next time."

"You did a fabulous job helping Jasmine to plan this wedding," said Whitney as she gave her a hug. "Everything is so beautiful."

Alyson rested her head against her sister's for a moment. "Thanks."

"I'll be back in a minute. Before the father-daughter dance," Whitney said before disappearing into the crowd.

"Look up," a familiar voice whispered into her ear.

She didn't bother to look around. She already recognized the strong arms that wrapped themselves lightly around her, careful not to squeeze too tight as he healed from his injuries. She looked up at the mistletoe that hung over her head, and Samson kissed her lips. Not a peck, like before. He kissed her deeply, and she kissed him back.

"What a nice surprise," she said.

Alyson and Samson swayed to the music. Her heart was filled with joy.

While Jasmine danced with their father, Alyson spotted Jennifer Madison across the room. Jennifer gave her an apologetic smile. Alyson had invited her weeks before, but after discontinuing her relationship with Madison, she expected that Jennifer would cut all ties with her—including removing her from the property on Abaco.

After the two made eye contact, Jennifer made a beeline for Alyson.

"Do you have a moment?" she asked. "I know this isn't the best time, but I really need to talk to you."

"You're right, it's not the best time," Alyson said.

"I owe you an apology," said Jennifer. "An apology for such grave behavior and corruption. My father had no idea that these things were going on in his company. He has been so far removed for a long time, and I've finally convinced him to let me help run Madison. My first order of business has been removing about 80 percent of his staff and replacing them."

"Really?" Alyson said.

"You'll be happy to know that Dustin was the first to go." Jennifer smiled. "We've hired all new people. Ethical people."

"That's good to know."

"I'd really like for you to continue to handle my father's commercial developments in Florida. If you're still interested in doing business with us."

Alyson was overjoyed by the proposition, but remained cool. "Okay."

"I'm sure I speak for my father when I say we wouldn't trust those properties to anyone else, Alyson. You're in a class all by yourself," Jennifer said. "What do you say?"

"What about the vacation property on Abaco? Am I still the listing agent?"

"Unfortunately, your services aren't needed for that property anymore. We sold that property yesterday."

"Really?"

"Of course you'll still earn the commission from the sale," said Jennifer.

"Who's the buyer?"

"Should I tell her or will you?" Jennifer asked Samson.

"I bought Madison House," said Samson.

"You got money like that?" Alyson asked.

"You're the one who insisted that I was broke." Samson laughed. "It was the kitchen that sold me. Not for me, but for you."

"Are you serious right now?" asked Alyson.

"Yes, love." He embraced her and waited for her to contain herself.

"So that means you're staying on the islands?"

"At least until I figure out what our future holds."

Jennifer interrupted the lovers. "What do you say about Madison Development?" she asked.

"I'm trying to get myself together. All of this is overwhelming."

"We'll talk next week," Jennifer said. "Drop by my office, and we'll talk about it." Jennifer extended her hand to Alyson. "I look forward to hearing from you soon."

Alyson shook her hand. Life had certainly taken a surprising turn.

Alyson rested in a chair next to Samson. They each sipped on flutes of champagne and watched as Jasmine smashed cake into Jackson's face. They laughed as Whitney nearly broke her neck trying to catch Jasmine's bouquet. As the group of women piled onto the floor in a scuffle for the flowers, it was Bijou who ascended with the coveted bouquet and waved it in the air.

"Looks like she got the bouquet," said Samson.

"But she didn't get the man. Not my man, anyway." Alyson gave Samson a warm smile.

"Not that you ever had anything to worry about."

Later, loud Caribbean music filled the night air. People in wild, outlandish and brightly colored costumes danced along Bay Street. Cheers and whistles drowned out any hopes of conversation among the guests. Drums were beat and horns were blown as every islander and guest enjoyed Junkanoo on Harbour Island. The annual street parade began promptly at one o'clock in the morning the day after Christmas, on Boxing Day. Junkanoo was a nice encore to Jasmine's beautiful wedding celebration.

"Nothing like this ever happens in Chicago," said Samson as he squeezed Alyson's hand.

"Chicago has its own special elements of Christmastime," said Alyson. "The snow is beautiful when you look at it from the inside. I could, however, get used to the frigid cold as long as I've got someone to keep me warm. I did some research. There's a nice real estate market there, and once my man becomes mayor..."

"You would consider relocating to Chicago?"

"If it means I get to spend my life with you, I'll go anywhere."

"That's sweet." He kissed her lips. "But I was thinking I might like to live somewhere warmer—like Miami. Build a career there."

"You would move to Florida?"

"I only want to be where you are, love."

"What about your new vacation home on Abaco?"

"I say we sail there tonight. Fix ourselves a nice Bahamian meal. Take a long walk along the beach, watch the sunset..."

"And after the vacation ends?"

"Who says it has to end?"

"We both have careers."

"You've been commuting between the islands and Miami anyway. So continue."

"What about you? What about your mayoral campaign?"

"I've had my eye on a few investment properties on the island of Abaco. Thought I'd purchase them, have my buddy Jackson renovate them. Then I'd hire a beautiful Realtor to get them on the market for me. You know any beautiful Realtors?"

"I know one, but she doesn't come cheap."

"Does she work on the barter system?"

"Possibly." She grinned. "Depends on what you're bartering."

"Love," he said emphatically.

"Hmm. How much is that worth?"

"More than any commission you'd ever earn."

"Okay, what else?"

"My love's not enough?"

"I make a pretty good commission. You'd have to step up your game."

"How about marriage and a lifetime of happiness?"

Alyson placed a fingertip on her chin, as if she was contemplating his offer.

"I don't come cheap. I'm high maintenance, and I like nice things."

"I know."

"And what about kids? Are you expecting some of those, too?"

"Absolutely! At least two or three. And one of them should be a girl that looks just like you."

"But not too soon. I have a career, and I'm not quite ready for my body to be all disproportioned."

"Sooner rather than later," he stated. "I'm ready to start a family."

"You drive a hard bargain. But I think we might be able to work something out."

"Good. We need a formal agreement."

"Should I have Jules draw something up?"

"No, we won't need Jules for this." He leaned down and kissed her lips. Pulled her close. "We'll sign this agreement later tonight."

"I love the sound of that."

In a short time, Samson had come into her life and re-arranged it. She'd vowed never to return to the Bahamas long-term, but she'd quickly learned that some vows were meant to be broken. She'd been afraid to give too much of her heart to any one man, but Samson was now demanding her trust.

As she stood on Bay Street and leaned her head against his chest, she closed her eyes and knew that when she opened them again, the man of her dreams would still be standing there, holding her and loving her fears away.

* * * * *

Everyone in the room turned at the same time.
Gianna Martelli stood in the doorway, a bright smile
painting her expression. Donovan pushed himself up
from his seat, a wave of anxiety washing over him.
Gianna met his stare, a nervous twitch pulsing at the edge
of her lip. Light danced in her eyes as her gaze shifted
from the top of his head to the floor beneath his feet and
back, finally setting on his face.

Donovan Boudreaux was neatly attired, wearing a
casual summer suit in tan-colored linen with a white dress
shirt open at the collar. Brown leather loafers completed
his look. His dark hair was cropped low and close, and
he sported just the faintest hint of a goatee. His features
were chiseled, and at first glance she could have easily
mistaken him for a high fashion model. Nothing about

him screamed teacher. The man was drop-dead gorgeous, and as she stared, he took her breath away.

The moment was suddenly surreal, as though everything was moving in slow motion. As she glided to his side, Donovan was awed by the sheer magnitude of the moment, feeling as if he was lost somewhere deep in the sweetest dream. And then she touched him, her slender arms reaching around to give him a warm hug.

"It's nice to finally meet you," Gianna said softly. "Welcome to Italy."

Donovan's smile spread full across his face, his gaze dancing over her features. Although she and her sister were identical, he would have easily proclaimed Gianna the most beautiful woman he'd ever laid eyes on. The photo on the dust jacket of her books didn't begin to do her justice. Her complexion was dark honey, a sun-kissed glow emanating from unblemished skin. Her eyes were large saucers, blue-black in color, and reminded him of vast expanses of black ice. Her features were delicate, a button nose and thin lips framed by lush, thick waves of jet-black hair that fell to midwaist on a petite frame. She was tiny, almost fragile, but carried herself as though she stood inches taller. She wore a floral-print, ankle-length skirt and a simple white shirt that stopped just below her full bustline, exposing a washboard stomach. Gianna Martelli was stunning!

*Don't miss*
*TUSCAN HEAT by Deborah Fletcher Mello,*
*available January 2016 wherever*
*Harlequin® Kimani Romance™*
*books and ebooks are sold.*

# REQUEST YOUR FREE BOOKS!

## 2 FREE NOVELS PLUS 2 FREE GIFTS!

**KIMANI** ROMANCE ™

### Love's ultimate destination!

KROM15

*Opposites attract...*
*and ignite!*

# PHYLLIS BOURNE

## *Heated Moments*

When she's dumped as the face of Espresso Cosmetics, Lola Gray hits the road. When a speeding ticket gets her in trouble in a small town in Ohio, the only bright spot is the hunky local police chief. Dylan Cooper relishes the peace and quiet of Cooper's Place. Now the stunning tabloid beauty he is holding for questioning is charming his hometown and seducing him. Will their sizzling affair become a lifetime of love?

## ESPRESSO EMPIRE

*Available December 2015!*

"A memorable tale of letting go of the past and taking risks. The characters are strong, relatable and will inspire readers to carve their own place in history." —*RT Book Reviews* on *SWEETER TEMPTATION*

### HARLEQUIN®
www.Harlequin.com

KPPB431215